Jennifer

JENNIFER LINDBERG

Printed in the United States of America

Library of Congress Control Number: 2020906860
ISBN: Softcover   978-1-64908-101-8
          Hardback   978-1-64908-102-5
          eBook   978-1-64908-100-1

Republished by: PageTurner Press and Media LLC
Publication Date: 05/22/2020

To order copies of this book, contact:

PageTurner Press and Media
Phone: 1-888-447-9651
order@pageturner.us
www.pageturner.us

Contents

Chapter 1

Storm of 1978

I was the last person born on the spit of the Red River. Red River was a small village of 225 Aleuts. The population grew to over 2,000 people when the summer season would start. It was a busy, vibrant village because of all the canneries and tanneries that lined the Red River. Red River salmon was sold all over the world during this time. Fox and seal furs were also exported from Red River to be worn across the globe.

I can only recall a few memories of the old village. I remember ruining a new pair of leather boots. Hot sunny days filled with picking berries. Village picnic's where everyone went and played all sorts of games. Most of these memories just sort of faded away. I do recall one particular memory that would be seared into my brain forever.

In the early 1900's a suspension bridge was constructed to connect the village to the canneries and tanneries. The bridge was an amazing piece of art, every time I walked across this bridge it was exciting. The Red River ran so fast that you could not cross over from the village to the canneries even though it was less than 400 feet across.

When the storm of 1978 began my Grandma Heidi had sent my Dad and one of my Uncle's to the store on the cannery side for supplies. We woke up to the wind howling. The wind just kept getting more intense as the morning passed by slowly.

I was watching from my Grandma Heidi's window when the storm ripped the bridge to pieces into the swift flowing Red River! That morning there were 3 people on the bridge with my Dad and Uncle Jack when it started to twist and buckle to our horror.

As soon as it started, Uncle Jack froze just under halfway over. You could see his confusion to continue or turn back. The others all went to the cannery side and were beckoning to Uncle Jack to move in one direction or another. All the while the bridge buckled and twisted. Finally, he could move and started for the cannery side. It went very slow as he tried to run over halfway. I could see it twisting and parts began to fall off into the swift moving Red River. Just as Uncle Jack made it to the cannery side it finally snapped one of the suspension cables and it blew apart into the Red River!

That storm destroyed the bridge, the store and the whole livelihood of the Red River salmon canneries. The storm of 1978 changed Red River, the people, the salmon and the rest of the salmon eating world. We no longer had a bridge to Across. Across the river is where they had school and many families. It was only a matter of time that the canneries and the store decided it was too great a loss to rebuild.

I remember one birthday my family surprised me with a big wheel. I couldn't believe it! My brother and I stood there just gazing at it. So new and for me! As soon as we got over the shock Brother Henry went over to it and ripped the tassels off the end of the handlebars and said that it didn't need them. We had a boardwalk system that run from the houses to the church. So, you could either go towards my Auntie Dana's direction or the other direction to the church with this wonderful wheeled toy.

One day I didn't want to nap and took off out of the house barefoot with Auntie Janet chasing me. I jumped on my big wheel and pedaled fast to get away laughing because I was being chased by Auntie Janet. I was halfway down the boardwalk and turned to see if auntie was still chasing me and I crashed off the boardwalk at the highest point off the ground. I remember falling into the pushkies and burners. I saw Aunt Janet coming for me and then I hit two big rocks on my head. I had put my feet down to try and stop me from going off the boardwalk and got a wood splinter about half an inch wide and the whole length of my foot. I was knocked out for three days! When I woke up, I still had to get splinters out of my right foot. I don't think we had the big wheel anymore.

Red River village is at the foot of the best mountains in the world to climb. We climbed four of them in the summer months. The first one on the edge of a cliff. The second one is rounded. The third one is the most climbed. The fourth was the steepest.

Chapter 2

Our Mountains

The whole village would climb the first mountain to have a picnic and play games. We would all have to at one point during the picnic look over the edge to certain death. Always there were jokesters ready to scare you about the edge.

The second mountain was rounded and had Rock People! This mountain also had the biggest patch of blackberries you ever seen. One summer my grandma Heidi and Erin wanted to get these yummy berries but needed a kid to go with them. I volunteered with a shout and a jump in the air. Rock People was all I could think of. ROCK PEOPLE! Rock People are part of a legend of long ago. When someone passed on and was loved and respected the living would go and build a Rock Person to remember and honor the person in life. You can still see them today. Grandma Heidi and Erin got lunch together with some fresh water and berry pickers. Away we went! We got to the top and it looked like a giant had picked all day, then spilled them all over the top of this mountain without picking them up.

4

Grandma Heidi had these berry pickers that all we had to do was rake this wonderful device on the patch and like magic it filled the bag full of yummy blackberries. After lunch we went visited and prayed for the Rock People. They were legends! I was moved by the look and feel of these long-ago people of Red River. My little village had important people in it and had been immortalized to be Rock People. I slowly walked up to the first one and noticed that they were old with lichen and moss on them. This is what kept them standing. They were simple figures of rock piled up to look like a person standing. These Rock People had stood there for years. You could almost imagine their life story being told while they were being built. What were their greatest accomplishments to be venerated after death? There were several about 15 or so Rock People standing there all looking at the village. How did these Rock People survive the storms, earthquakes and test of time? Awe is all I could think of on the way down that mountain full of berries and of an ancient time.

The third mountain in from the ocean that we would climb had a wishing well at the top. This was the mountain that was most climbed because it was the easiest one to climb. Except at the very top 200 feet or so. This always made me uneasy and feel like I could just roll off this mountain with one wrong step. I always felt like I was walking where my people before me walked. The path to the top of the mountain was well defined and took many steps to make this path. On a beautiful clear day you could see several smoking volcanoes on the mainland. Volcanic ash was spread all across the sky in long lines that sometimes blended together to make one long ash cloud. Looking out across behind the mountain was always so rewarding, we made it to see the backside of the mountains, incredible!

The fourth mountain looked like it came straight up from the bottom of the ocean with how steep it was compared to the other three. Most of the mountain was all rock with the bottom half covered in vegetation. We did not climb this mountain unless we had a large group.

One summer afternoon we climbed the fourth mountain to pick berries on the way down. My youngest Brother Victor came bursting through the door to drag me to climb the mountain. My Dad had made pancakes for breakfast and rolled them up with peanut butter and jelly, my favorite snack for hiking! Oh, yeah with jars of hot tea and water. Away we went! We caught up with the rest of the group at the foot of the mountain. We felt like we were about to ascend Mount Everest. This mountain is rockier to climb than the others. When we got halfway up I was thinking we have to come back this way but down and tired. The trail has been there for a long time. A beaten down path carved into a mountain we barely climb. Many, many generations of walking this path has made it what it is today. We went through the thick alders to a creek that felt like a small waterfall. Felt like an old trail to get to ancient grounds. We made it to the top without any problems. Being on top of this mountain was breathtaking, it is almost the highest peak.

We had a picnic then some games like hide and seek, not it and how far can you throw a rock off the mountain. Tired and ready to go back to the village we start down Mount Everest. We got through the creek waterfall to come out into the open to pick berries on the way down. We usually had a coffee can tied to a string. Mine did not have the string through it and I dropped my can. It took off on a race to the bottom of the mountain. I chased after it for about a hundred feet or so and decided that it would wait for me at the bottom. But at this point I had separated myself from the group, not good!

About halfway down the mountain there was a patch of alders about 50 feet wide. I was walking slowly waiting for the group to catch up to me so we could hit the berry bushes at the same time. I turned to look up at them, the patch of alders in the center started to sway back and forth vigorously. Those moments when you try to recall "this is what you do when you come across a brown bear". What everyone tells you while you are safe and sound at home. First thought is to not run! But your feet want to save you when danger is near.

I was not the first one to start running, they were! Of course, they were closer to the brown bear than I was. We all seen the bushes sway back and forth again, they all took off at the same time towards me! I was thinking don't run, but my feet seen others run and took off down the side of the mountain before my brain could think of anything else.

Now when you run down a steep, grassy, hilly mountain you kind of like got super powers. One leap felt like sixteen feet in one stride. We were afraid of this huge 20-foot-tall, 2,000-pound angry bear after us for disturbing his afternoon nap! So, we are running full out down the mountain with a bear chasing us, or so we imagined. We run until we were all so exhausted. We stopped out of breath counting everyone. No one was left behind, whew! It turned out the bear didn't even come out of the alders to chase us. So, we went about picking salmonberries and return to the village.

Chapter 3

Village beliefs

In the old village of Red River, the Russian Orthodox Church had built one in Red River. I believe it was completed in June of 1886. The colors of the church was light green and white with three onion domes. I am sure it is held together by paint and the spiders holding hands! I always thought the church was beautiful.

Pretty much every church service we went to involved lit candles. Most of the time they were in front of their holy pictures, sometimes they armed us with lit candles in rows of people. I wondered about these things because the only water in sight was in a kettle boiling on the wood stove. None the less no flaming accidents occurred while I went to church.

Going to church was one of the craziest things we did. Let's start out with Easter! Just coming out of winter Easter would happen. Lent was a quiet time for the village. Lent would start 40 days before Easter we would attend church to start the forgiving of our sins. I was not sure what sins were, but they were to repent their sins.

The church sits on top of a cliff overlooking the ocean to the "Valley of 10,000 Smokes". Beautiful spot for a church. Being on top of a hill though, we had to climb stairs to get to it. Two sets of stairs brought you to a "Y" that led to the church. The first set of stairs are the ones up on top of a hill that almost went straight up like a ladder, almost! The other set of stairs were for the people that lived near the ocean. This set was long and not so steep as the other. Either staircase you chose to use was breathtaking on any day.

During Lent we were not to be loud, argue or sin! The closer we got to Easter the services would begin. The church was decorated in black. You couldn't eat meat, dairy products, chew gum or eat raised dough products. We all stayed home and waited for Easter to come. A week before Easter the pussy willows and plants would start to bud. Every time we had a service the adults would have to kneel 40 times before the service would start. It was because they "sinned"! Good Friday was a big start of the week leading up to Easter. Midnight Service was at 11pm until 3 or 4, depending on who the priest was. All the sinners would do their kneeling before this time, so service can start on time.

Just before midnight we would grab holy pictures with some crosses and head out into the night to circle the church three times. My candle never seemed to get blown out by the wind. Upon completion of the circling of the church we would stand at the door and sing. Then, as if by magic when we entered all the black was gone and brightness had replaced it all. Nothing short of a miracle! We would continue midnight service with lit candles. One time I fell asleep with a lit candle! After the service we were released to go home and celebrate. Traditional foods to be eaten and let sinning begin once again!

Chapter 4

School

When I was old enough to attend school, it was held at the spit of the Red River. I enjoyed school so much I tried to go every day. Mr. Watson was my first schoolteacher, wonderful person and an excellent teacher. We had new teachers every year from all over the country. Some had kids with them, others had grown children. We were all amazed at what stories they had to tell.

With the new school there were different opportunities available to us. One of the many teachers that came through thought we needed a band and study the bible. This schoolteacher had a farm back down south. When the new school year started, he had ordered chickens, snakes, spiders, and crickets to the village. These creatures were so amazing, we got to feed them and care for them.

When the band instruments came in, we had no idea what to do with them. When we entered the gym, they were all set up with stands and chairs. He said to pick one and that would be ours to practice with during the school year. Trumpets, flutes, horns and clarinets for us to choose from. We were in awe and stared in amazement. My

Brother and I had picked the clarinet to learn. Unfortunately, my fingers were too small to play the real low notes. Brother could play those notes well.

Red River storms were crazy at times because we lived on the end of an island. One such storm had everyone scared of what changes it could bring. The storm of 78' took out our bridge and canneries. We went to Erin's place to check on her and her husband. When we got there everyone was excited about this stick controlled by the devil. They said this stick had knocked people down and hit others. This flying stick controlled by the devil had them all running inside to hide. I raced over to the window to see this flying stick, nothing!

A new site was being cleared away the next summer for the Hud housing we were going to get. All these materials started to come in on barges for the new site. Rumors that they were going to build a new village further up the Red River.

Chapter 5

Bears and the Boogeyman

Bears and the boogeyman were up there as far as we were concerned. So, we did not understand why they wanted us there. Scary! Near the end of that first summer the new site was well under construction. They needed young people to watch the new site from robbers and thieves. There are no robbers and thieves in this village we thought. The construction people insisted on having two week shifts through the winter and they would pay them. They came back with stories about their shift watch, I was too young to hear these scary tales.

Two buildings at the new site is where they set up camp for the winter. We were too young to go and see the construction site. We were not allowed where men were working and making money. Adult stuff!

The following spring, we seen the most peculiar sight of half-built houses on barges. One was red and another was blue, how could they build half houses we thought. Always they came back with stories of little people and something about a creek with a hole in the ground next to it. Boogeyman they would say.

I don't remember the day we moved to the new site, but one family at a time moved to a brand-new modular house. Our family and like many others were now divided up between these new modular houses. My Dad, brother Henry and I moved into a two-bedroom modular house on the lower side of the village. Grandma Heidi and the rest of them moved into a two-bedroom just up the hill from us. Most had families out of Red River and moved. No canneries and no school had made people move to make money. Population of Red River had dropped dramatically. I never thought of what would happen to those abandoned houses after we moved into new digs, a lot had changed for us and others were still the same. New place was wonderful, we still did not have running water or electricity yet.

My Dad worked odd jobs that came to Red River, all seasonal work. One of the locals didn't move into the new village, he had a nice little cabin he was happy with. He had a sport fishing lodge and made a nice living. Every year he would leave to be with his wife down south. He said he liked the fishing and enjoyed going to the city for winter. I remember one visit I had stayed to listen about the city life, he talked my dad into starting a fishing lodge for himself. My Dad transformed the back outside entrance into a little bedroom with bunkbeds and carpet. We had some clients that following summer and continued to grow in numbers for a maximum of 20 clients a week at peak season.

Early in the spring there is a red run of salmon. We would go and set the seine out at the point to catch 300-600 fish. You had to have several people together to pull the seine to the beach. First, you set out the net with the skiff and hold hook for about 10 minutes and start to slowly close the net. The beach seine crew on the beach needed to hold the seine in place and help close the set. Pull and grab until it was closed. The fun part is to pick the fish species that you wanted out and let the rest go. They would select the fish they wanted; one haul usually got enough salmon to preserve for the winter.

With a full skiff they would head to the beach just below the house so they wouldn't have far to pack the five gallon buckets up to the smoking and drying area. The fish filleting would began. My Dad and Uncles were so fast and proficient at this task, it only took a couple of hours. The seagulls would all be in an uproar singing ka-de-uk, ka-de-uk we will eat what you discard. So noisy! They packed them in buckets to lay out next to the smoke house to salt. After soaking in rock salt, they would rinse in saltwater from the river. The younger guys had to climb up the steepest stairway with buckets of saltwater to rinse the fish to hang. Then, they would hang the fish to start smoking for two weeks.

My family has this process down and it is so delicious. I remember when it was done, they would cut up several to sample for lunch. Throughout this day we would see most of the villagers. Cold hard smoked salmon is what my family would do every year. We would also put salmon up to dry. You had to get the first run of reds to beat the black flies' arrival. Black flies would lay eggs in the soft meat. Hopefully you put your fish up before then, they could destroy the whole batch.

Most times I had to go with my Brother Henry, so he wasn't alone, the drying racks were across the creek and a little bit of a hike up the hill. When it rained you had to turn every pair, so the skin side was out, to stop moisture. The drying racks held 300 pairs of salmon. It was a basic structure with tin for a roof, open sides with fish net draped over it to keep out animals. Dry fish is my favorite way to eat salmon, yum!

Chapter 6

A new Ma

Every year in town at the end of the school year they had a festival, for five days. Fun, food, friends and family all in five days. Old Wives Tales said if your palm itches you will get money. If your eye twitches you will see someone you have not seen in a long time. If you hit your elbow you were going to travel. All these should happen if you were going to the festival. Many activities were available during this time. You could bet on real live rat races, crab legs for cheap, take a spin on the many carnival rides.

Trappers could sell their pelts that they worked so hard to get ready for this gathering. Many fine pelts of fox, seal and weasels were available for purchase. Every day they had different activities for children, the one I looked forward to the most was the sawdust pile with hundreds of dollars in real silver dollars in it. There were many side shows and contests for all ages. Activities for the adults to enter were foot races, arm wrestling contest and the most watched event was the Survival Suit race. So, every year you could afford to go, you went!

This one year after we moved to the new site I felt like it was important to go to the festival. I was told no we didn't have the money to go, bummed! I begged and bugged for a week before the start of the festival. Every day I would plead to go to town. I was going if I had to walk, I told Dad. A day before it was time to go on the plane my Dad said he got the money to go but… we did not care But! We were going! Wahoo! Okay we calmed down to hear "But" we had to camp at the beach, because the hotels were filled up. Still did not care, we were going!

When we got to town we checked the hotel and they had a room, yes! We had a great first day and were exhausted. When we woke up the next morning our whole world had changed. A woman was in bed with my dad and she was giggling and laughing saying that she did not know my dad had kids. She was a beautiful Filipino woman. Shocked and amazed we just stared. Betty!

The Festival we were so excited for was a blur after we met Betty. Betty was a beautiful, colorful, happy looking woman. My dad was taken by this woman and she came back to the village with us.

My Ma, Selma, had died of a heart attack when I was about two years old. Dad was still in college and had four kids to watch suddenly. We were split up at this point, my older brother Henry and I stayed with my dad's family. My older Sister Holly with my younger Brother Victor were given to my mom's side of the family. We still lived in the same village, but we were in two different worlds.

First thing I remember when we returned from the festival was Betty's cooking. My dad over the years had cooked for us, but most meals were at my grandma's. My grandma used only so many spices and, in the village, there is no store. Most of the time the food was bland, I am not complaining, I like it that way. The real flavor of the meat comes out. Betty had put stuff like garlic, basil leaves, peppercorns and vinegar in the foods she cooked. Oh, yeah who could forget the soy sauce! Betty had got all the ingredients for egg rolls. Hamburger ones! She prepped the ingredients then had us help her roll egg rolls for dinner and the rest of the week.

Fun! A new Ma, new food and only we could understand her. Betty talked real fast and we had to train our ears to listen faster. A month went by and we could translate to others what she had just said.

We thought it was so strange that someone could talk straight English and we couldn't understand her. So much fun! Accent and her way of pointing with her lips a nod in one direction or say over der. She would say "Oih" to get your attention, then point with her lips. So funny!

We totally accepted Betty into our lives. I am sure at one point we didn't let her into our worlds because she was new. My dad and Betty went to town to buy stuff for her to live in the village and groceries. When they came back Betty had surprises for us. We were kids and kids misbehave and act up towards their parents. This one time after they came back from town Betty had a plan. Smart woman! Very smart! Impressive! When she noticed we were not into having a new Ma and all she whipped out this dart board and gathered my Brother Henry and I together. She stated that kids our age had already mastered small weapons for protection and hunting. Weapons! Weapons was all we heard, oh yeah let's see it! Betty had gotten throwing stars, nun-chuks and a dart board. She demonstrated for us and wow Betty was a star throwing, nun-chuk swinging, crazy cooking Mama! Wow! My dad had come home that day to holes in the walls, elbows bruised and wild-eyed kids. We were ninja's, no doubt!

Betty wanted halibut one day, Dad set it up the next nice day for Uncle Charles to take us jigging. We were out there for about an hour, nothing! Then I got a tug! I was excited, I got it to the side, Uncle Charles could see before us. I asked what it was, he just laughed and said just pull it over the side, so I yanked the line and this huge ugly, red, pokey, round fish flew at Betty and I. Crazy! We were hollering as it flew over us and it dropped to the bottom of the skiff. "Red snapper" Uncle Charles said.

Chapter 7

Jennifer The Pilot

In life I believe you only get one good dog; Luke was that for me. I brought home this black puppy with a white spot on his chest. I did not ask my dad if I could have him or not. I saw this black puppy that my friends' parents were giving away and I latched onto him, my Dad could not refuse me. My Dad is so awesome, he built this little half a house attached to the side of the house.

Luke had whined and howled for 3 nights, my Dad knew I would try to let him in and stopped me every time I tried to let him in. "No, he must know his place in this family". Dad would say when I would cry to let him in. Animals are to stay outside; they are animals and are built to stay outdoors. Simple! On the fourth night Luke decided that his own house and living with us was not so bad and decided to stay. Luke never tried to enter the house or expected to go in. My dog was smart and jealous. Grandma Heidi had a small Germen Shepard looking dog named Chipper. Chipper liked Luke and trained him to be a good dog.

Our life was complete we had a house, a Mom and a Dad, and a new dog to go with it all. Strange how life gives you all this and takes away some. In my kid world we had it all. The school only could educate you until you hit high school. A couple of options at this point, go to town, correspondence or go far away to a boarding school. Brother Henry one day had to get on a plane and go to an Indian boarding school in another state. I had no idea this was to happen. My brother was being pushed to get ready to travel and be gone for the school year. The school year! I couldn't imagine a life without my brother. He had turned into an adult in two minutes it seemed and then he was out of my world. Devastated, a life without brother! Unimaginable!

Two weeks later I was helping Grandma Heidi and Aunt Janet get ready to move to town. The plane was on its way and my Grandma was running around looking for this piece of paper called Medicaid. I found it under the bed and gave it to them. They were excited and acting crazy. The plane flew in and they were getting ready to leave their house when they stopped and looked at me and said come on let's go. I am like let's go where? They simply said that I was to go with them and go to school. What? I told them that I had not packed and have no clothes to go to town. My Aunt Janet was throwing wet clothes in bags and said we would get me some clothes in town. Town was beautiful and sunny when we landed.

Living in town was a new adventure. My brother Henry was attending school over 2,000 miles away for high school and I was in town going to middle school. My Dad and Betty were all alone in Red River. School was school except I was in the middle of white people. I had made a couple of friends right away. We were quite a sight; I am sure of it. Amy was tall, creamy white with fiery red hair. Rita was tall white and beautiful blonde hair. I was short, brown skinned and native. Karen was just taller than me with beautiful copper colored, wavy hair. We got along well, and Amy was the first friend I ever invited to my birthday. School was a blur with all the class changes and a locker I couldn't get into half the time, I just carried all my books.

What was most interesting about this period in my life was I had to fly back and forth to the village to see my Dad. Like I said before native children were spoiled. We wanted to do something we were given the tools or knowledge to do them. Chad "The Pilot" was the pilot I had gotten on most of my trips. At Christmas break I went to the village and was getting ready to return to school. Chad The Pilot was all set to take off or so I thought. Chad had pulled out his lunch box declaring that he was hungry, and I was to fly the plane! He said he had full confidence in me that I flew enough I could fly us to town. Given instructions on how to start and taxi down the runway, I took ahold of the yoke and listened very carefully as I taxied down the runway as he instructed how to lift off the ground. In life sometimes you must take the yoke and go for it! Wow, what a feeling! I was flying the plane! With a little bit more instruction and pointed in the direction of town Chad took a nap. It was beautiful and calm that day I flew to town. Incredible! As we neared town, I woke Chad up and he instructed how to land, we landed perfectly.

Chapter 8

Jennifer

School was over and the following year my sister Holly was enrolled at the Indian boarding school along with my Brother Henry. Henry had come back to Red River with so many stories of the city. Places were open 24 hours a day! You could eat fries at 2 in the morning! Awesome! I could not wait for high school to start for me. During the time that I went to town for school my Dad had moved into my Grandma's 4-bedroom house. This move was to help the expansion of his sportfishing lodge. So, when we returned it was to a new house, so big for us I thought. But I did get my own room.

The new house was near the dump and in the fall many bears hit the dump to fatten up for their winter's sleep. Bears have a big circle of food that they keep doing all summer, depending on how big their circle was, we seen most bears every 7-10 days. Bears have a good memory for easy getting food, the dump was everyone's favorite. When the locals would dump in bear season they pulled up and honked a couple of times, waited for the bears to go in the bushes then get out, dump, and get back in and drive off. From my bedroom window you could see all this happen. When someone said there was a bear in the

21

village, I always went home. I am not about to find out if they were full or hungry! To this day I always go in the other direction of these massive animals.

When I had graduated the eighth grade my Dad had talked to me about how life was when you were an adult. He had stated that kids' played with dolls and boats. I was growing into an adult he stated and therefore I was to put down these kid games. My Dad said that my childhood name "Jenny" was to be no more, my adult name was "Jennifer" and I was to tell everyone. My life just felt different after that conversation, an adult! Throughout that summer my Dad had taken the time to explain in great detail all the questions I had about becoming an adult.

In the fall was the time Brother Henry and I would go to a place called The Swimming Hole to get giant wood logs for our winter supply of firewood. My Grandma's foyer could hold at least 5 cords of wood. Red cedar and yellow cedar were used for king-a-ling. My Dad would watch for the fine weather to go to The Swimming Hole because we had to go out to the ocean and travel for about ten minutes on the open water for the perfect spot to pull logs off the beach. Baseball sized rocks led to a steep drop off into the ocean, perfect to get the skiff right on the beach. My Sister Holly came with us a couple of times. The first day my Sister Holly and I planned on swimming in the ocean. We had our village swim-ware, shorts and a t-shirt. Ready and heading for the water, my Brother states as we near the water that he wouldn't swim there because of the sealions. Sealions! We did not think of that at all, no swimming for us.

We would take about three days to collect wood logs to drag back to the village. Then, the work would begin for the rest of us. At the beach the men would cut up the logs into sections to bring to the house. When it got to the house, they started to chop it up and make a pile of wood perfect for king-a-ling. That was my job, I was set up with a small stool and a chopping block. My Brother showed me how to chop up these boards for king-a-ling. Hours and hours turned into days of chopping king-a-ling. The foyer would fill up with regular chopped wood and right in front was my hard work on display. A wall of king-a-ling! The house smelled so good, red cedar and yellow cedar! We had two houses and one banya to burn all through the winter. Hot, cold and visions of warm fire went through my head every year.

Chapter 9

Freshman Year

My freshman year had arrived with great anticipation, I was to attend the Indian high school. This year my Dad had to enroll three of his kid's into high school. My Sister Holly and I were good at playing volleyball. The school had a sports camp that started two weeks before school started. My Sister and I headed out early for this camp. Up to this point I had flown in small planes and even been a pilot once, but I had never been on a big plane or to the huge airports. My Sister had traveled the year before and knew what to do.

I was not pre-pared for the heat, Red River on a hot day reached maybe 70 degrees with the cool ocean breeze. Whew! Hot! We had staff on their way to pick us up. No meeting point or set up time to be at a certain place or nothing. My Sister Holly and I had been at this airport for hours now and new it from top to bottom. She felt confident enough to spit up and look for the staff separately.

At 1 a.m. I was scanning the crowd for this 6'4" guy with glasses. When this 6'4" guy with glasses was on the second floor spied me. You could see the you look like the one I am looking for. I froze and he come down the steps asking if I was related to Holly. I said yes and we waited for Holly to come back to the meeting place and started to travel by van to the campus. I never been on a freeway before and we were flying down the road 55 m.p.h. Wow! So many lights, I thought, why? We passed a Denny's and he asked if we wanted fries or a burger, my Sister immediately said "no" we were just going to go to sleep when we got to the dorms. I would have gone to Denny's just to eat something at 2 a.m. in the morning. When we arrived at the school we seen fields of grass, a water tower and a football field. Amazing! We got settled in for the night. I could not sleep much, too hot and the crickets were making so much noise. Holly woke me up the next day to get ready for the day. We headed to breakfast and then for a long day in the sun of volleyball practice.

At first my Sister and I were roommates in dorm 9. That lasted about two weeks, my Sister transferred me over to the smart people dorm 7. This was a co-ed dorm, that did not last long either. My Sister and I did not grow up together, so it was difficult to relate or get along. She said that I had to go be a freshman and make my own friends. Hmm, how do I make my own friends, I thought.

The very next day during Home-Economics the teacher gave us an assignment to get to know your classmates project. He said to pick a person to ask questions. Everyone at my table split except for Brad. We looked at each other and said I guess we get to ask each other questions. Logically I started out with what kind of Indian are you question, Brad stated he was a Sioux Indian. I wrote that down, Sue Indian! He looked at my paper and seeing I spelled Sioux wrong, him and Corey laughed and corrected me. Brad became my first friend my Sister told me to seek out. A couple of weeks went by and I noticed this native gal had pretty much the same classes and I started to sit by her and slowly started to talk to her. Amber was her name, so now I could report to my Sister I had made two friends. She rolled her eyes and said go make more, to this day I am not sure why she didn't like me. In the end it did force me to get out there more on my own and try.

High school was basically the same. English, math, science, home economics and gym were my favorites. I was in good health and in good shape in high school. I went to gym class and did the work outs for about a month. I noticed there was a pregnant gal and they made her do the work outs, I did not agree. So, I started to protest and not do the work outs and stated I work out on my own time. I stated that I did not need these grueling stupid exercises! The teacher did not know what to do with me and left me alone. About a week went by as I sat on the sidelines and the teacher was like you don't want to exercise, you can do laundry and clean. Done deal! She of course did not give me my gym credit. At the end of the semester she said that she never wanted to see me again as long as she worked there, I totally agreed.

There was a natural resources class that took up two class periods that I had signed up for. We learned about how useful trees were to the earth and went out and planted trees for the rest of the semester. It was so much fun! One hot afternoon we were going back to class when we heard this humming, it got louder the closer we got to the school building and then this huge dark cloud was heading toward us. Scary and loud! Suddenly, this dark cloud was upon us, bees on the move! So loud, we raced to get inside the school because bee stragglers started to check us out. No one was hurt but we were all out of breath.

Basketball was a popular sport that everyone supported. That basketball coach knew his job well. My Brother Henry was a good basketball player. With the coaches help he made him an exceptional ball player. That basketball coach took all them athletes from different places and melded them together to be winners. The basketball games were intense! The coach honed each individual player's skill and pushed them to their limits.

Wow, what a time to be at a home game. This home game we were playing got so loud and intense. The score was tied with seconds on the clock when we stole the ball and raced to our side of the court. With a pass to the inside man, he jumped and threw the ball for the shot. The ball circled three times, it had just about dropped in to just almost out of the basket. Everyone was standing trying to help the ball drop in for the shot, as the horn blew it slowly circled to drop in for the winning basket. Go team!

I really enjoyed being a spectator to all the home games. I was always busy and kept myself in excellent shape, but I did not join sports. I am not an athletic person.

So, Christmas time came and time to travel back to Red River for the two-week vacation. My Dad had moved to town for the winter.

We had stayed in a Filipino boarding house where you rent a room and share the rest of the house. We had tickets to Red River and wanted to go for the winter vacation. My Dad and Betty were going to stay in town for the school break, he said if we wanted to go home, he would order fuel and lights for us. My Uncle was in the village to keep an eye on us. With enough food to feed the village we headed to Red River the next day. Over the years we had all our meals cooked by adults and served to us. I cooked simple things like top ramen and canned foods before. Dad had known this and got us easy stuff to cook. We got to the house on Friday afternoon with barely any stove fuel. The flame was just enough to keep the place from freezing. Brother and I settled in and he said we should cook at least an hour before we would get hungry.

So, this is what happened on the first night. We had a coffee maker for hot water to make tea and cup o'noodles. We unpacked the food and Brother decided we should eat hot dogs and top ramen for dinner. Brother was busy in the room and hollered what I was to do to make the hot dogs. I heard him say to heat the water up in the coffee pot then put the dogs in the water. Simple, right! Hot water was done, I hollered what to do again. He said the same thing and I hollered are you sure? He said, "Jenny just do it", so I took the hot dogs out of the plastic and started to slide a hot dog in the coffee pot where you pour from. Just at that moment my friend Brandy comes around the corner and asks what are you doing? I felt a little funny sliding that hot dog in the pot anyways so when my friend Brandy came around the corner asking me what I was doing, I could only laugh at myself. Brother comes rushing into the kitchen to see what was so funny. He just said "Jenny" and shook his head back and forth laughing. I did not hear him say he put a pot over the burner and to put the hot water from the coffee maker in the pot on the stove. So funny, coffee dogs!

In the winter we had three hills to slide on when it wasn't slick with ice. One of these hills was just outside our house. When the nights were clear and still out my Brother and I would gear up to go sledding. We tried to get the other kids to go sliding at night, no one joined us. Sometimes we would get a couple of others to go but most nights we were by ourselves. Out of town on a beautiful clear winter night there are so many stars, I didn't know any of the names of the star constellations. The big dipper and the small dipper were about the only ones we knew for sure. Wow! Breathing the crisp cool air and seeing your breath float away into oblivion was awesome. The endless black sky with millions of stars twinkling back at us was incredible. The air is so clean you could taste and smell the ocean and the earth. Exhausted from sliding and climbing the hill we would just lay down in the snow to see what was out there in the endless display of stars. Sometimes we were lucky enough to see a shooting star or the northern lights.

Traveling back to school was always exciting, I had always loved to travel. I did not mind having layovers, it was time to see what airports were made of and what was in it. In the Seattle airport there were these chairs that had a small television attached to it. You put 25 cents in, it gave you a choice of 10-15 channels and fifteen minutes of viewing. Most of our flights into Seattle were at nighttime, so many lights. I used to think what a waste of so much electricity. We had no electricity when we grew up in the old village. We rose at daybreak and was close to bedtime by the time night fell. I could not believe so many people in one area working together to live life. I thought this is only one city, how many more out there just wasting electricity. Amazing!

The other students from the lower 48 traveled by train or bus. Large groups would join up at one point, then head to the campus for the second half of the school year.

There were two destinations for us student's to go and hang out on the weekends, The Mall uptown and The City Center. The public bus routes would take us there if we went to the local grocery store or Kmart. Taking the city bus was a new and great way to get somewhere without your own vehicle. We were far from home, far from places you can only get to on your own two feet. Living on village time my whole life, we could not seem to catch the last bus of the day. So you either pool together your dough and cab it or walk. We always came to the same conclusion, save my money and walk!

Walking back from the uptown Mall is a shorter walk than from The City Center, by a long shot. The hike back to campus from The Mall was on a straight away till you hit the local grocery store. Traffic and the smell of exhaust was new to us, most of the time we hit the backroads and took our time. Near the campus there was a playground we would hang out and rest before the final trek to campus. This had some swings and benches to rest on, if we were quiet!

When we were hiking back to campus from The City Center the route we always took was the railroad tracks, they went right past the old campus. I had seen trains on television and heard them from campus, but never actually seen one on the rails. Wow! When we heard a train coming, we would all check to see what kind of coins we had to smoosh on the tracks. Not too many though because you can't spend smooshed coins. We would spend the next half hour looking for our treasures you couldn't spend.

On our way again with our smooshed coins, we come across the old school cemetery. We went to look at the names on the headstones and found one that had written on it Davey Crockett. No fooling! Saw it with my own eyes. We would always say a prayer and be on our way. Next came a bridge, not a very long one, a train could come at any time and force us to jump or run. No train ever came at the right time, how rude!

Leaving behind the train tracks up come the old campus, the only buildings left were part of the clinic and the old cookhouse. My dad had gone to school here when these buildings were in use. Ancient!

I had heard many stories of students seeing sets of eyes in there at night. Of course, I got a group together to go see these buildings the next weekend. At night when you get closer to the old campus it gets quiet and eerie feeling. It almost felt like going back in time, your imagination leads you to old Indian grounds in and abandoned area.

First question, why is it abandoned by the Indians? Indians just don't abandon good grounds. Second question, why the heck are we out here at the corner of the campus with bad lighting? So, we get closer to the building we seen in the daylight a week ago and it does not look the same. Shadows are cast and windows are blackened with darkness. We went left to circle the creepy looking old clinic and came across a break in the fence.

Third question was seen across all our faces; do we dare go inside the perimeter? One of the girls stated she was too scared to go in and too scared to wait for us to explore. Some continued along the outside of the fence and kept an eye on the blackened windows. When we got out to the corner of the fence one of the guys hollered and said he seen a set of eyes in the basement between two boards. We stopped and looked when we saw them too! The girls took off running and screaming for the stadium. When the girls screamed, the set of eyes jumped out of the basement and turned into a cat. Ooh, man! We caught up to the group and had a good laugh, stray cats!

School would continue and near the end of the year the school would take us on field trips to the beach, parks, or to one of many different falls. I never heard of May Day until high school. Apparently, this is an unofficial holiday to start off the summer of adventures. Our very own gourmet cooks would pack up a wonderful spread for a large picnic. The teachers would participate and play games like softball, egg toss and horseshoe.

One year we headed to some beautiful falls. They had seven different falls, several huge picnic areas and a lake to float boats. So, we get there and check out to see what we wanted to do first. We had come around this corner that lead to the lake and came across this Russian family that offered us wine. Umm, no! Are you crazy is what we thought? In a minute about 300 Indians are going to come around that corner to see this Russian family.

This being the first time at the falls we headed to hike around the biggest fall there, the trail had gone under the fall and you could feel the spray on your face. We had gone the wrong way and had to hike back up the steepest part of the falls.

Summer break, no more books! The first summer break I spent in Red River. The second day I went to check the mail and one of the locals asked now that I knew what's out there, what do I think of Red River? It feels like I am in a box with no sides.

This summer Dad had decided we should have our own raft to go fishing. If we told where we were going, we could set sail. It was made of wood, weighted 200 pounds and was square. Like a floating box! My Younger Brother Victor, my cousin and I spent the summer buffing up our arms, yeah! We were tough at the end of that summer. I love fish and salmonberries. We were always busy, we had the fisherman's tan, brown from the wrist down and the neck up. Nothing too interesting happened that summer.

Fall came and time to head back to school, traveling was so much fun. The weather was so unpredictable in the fall so, we headed to town a couple of days before our scheduled flight. I would stay with family and then off to the big city. This year I was staying at my Aunt Stephanie's with my Sister Holly until it was time for us to travel back to school.

Holly had given me these directions to my Aunt Stephanie's house. Walk like you are going to Safeway, stay on the road till just past it. You will see a big brown house, go left down that street till you hit the road that goes right. Then take that right until you get to the trailer # 2. I will be outside waiting. I am like what? I was on a public phone downtown; she gets mad and says start walking now! Aah, okay! Walking and walking I see this big brown house, yes! Left then right and I will be at my Auntie's house, my Sister was sitting on the steps when I got there, whew! I did not get lost! A couple of days of good cooking, good company and lots of cribbage and partner's happening. I love my family! So, over my high school career I got to see a lot of family that I normally didn't get to see.

Chapter 10

Sophomore Year

Returning to school this year I was not a rookie, a veteran! Yeah! Initiation included the vets who were dicks would drag the new students through the mud when it rained. So not fair! I was approached by the biggest group of vets and seen that look; this is going to be fun. Not! I took off running like I just fell through the ice, gone. Someone got ahold of my coat and I just slipped out of it, they tried to taunt me with I have your coat and stuff in it. I laughed and said I have all the good stuff in my pants pockets, I am no fool! Keep my coat! I didn't participate in these initiations of rookies. I suggested to the new students not to go out when it rained if you don't want to be dragged in the mud. This year of school flew by with no incidents.

Christmas break was upon us faster than a speeding bullet. During the Christmas break we would go to collect some native foods from the outside beach called The cliffs. There were these huge rocks that fell from the cliff into the ocean and was perfect to grow ooh-he-ducks and oo-ducks. We would also collect blue mussels and whatever extra food we found. We could only collect these delicacies during the winter months with "r" in them. The elders would keep an eye on the tides for a good low tide during the day. We would get our gear on for cold wet weather, our five-gallon buckets and butter knives. A marching we would go to the outside beach with visions of the yummy sweet taste of fresh oo-ducks for all. We would get there during daylight and start prying the ooh-he-ducks off the rocks. We usually went to The cliffs a mile and a half from the village. The best strategy was to start at the edge of the water and slowly get pushed up the beach by the incoming tide. We stayed too long one time and night fall started. When it gets dark enough you can see the spark that the ooh-he-ducks put out. I didn't know they did that and they put on a spectacular show for us.

Time to travel back to school for the second half of my Sophomore year. This was a blur and went fast. This May Day celebration took part at a park on the other side of town that had a patch of woods. A couple of my friends and I headed into the woods to hike the trail, we did not time our return in time and came back to an empty parking lot. Left behind! Lucky for me my friends were from this town and knew their way around. Seasoned hitch-hikers they suggested we hitch back to campus, okay sounds good to me. We started out walking towards campus and had run into this young man that needed someone with a valid driver's license to get his Camaro. Fortunately for him and us my friend had one of these wonderful cards. Oh, yeah away we went in style back to campus.

That summer we spent living with my Aunt Janet and her kid's, my favorite cousins Elise and Brent. They were too young to hang out with us, that summer my aunt lived next to a lake, and we would go there every chance we got. I had a part time job working with the Native facility as a nighttime janitor. I really enjoyed working with the old man and had a blast cleaning the building.

Most days Brother Henry, cousin Adam and I would spend at the lake rafting on a homemade raft made from two 4x12's tied together. We just barely floated, if you moved too much the water would go over the top of the board. The lake has a small island in the middle of it with a couple of trees.

We would always try to make it around the whole lake, but never did. One day we attempted to cross over the middle and out of the blackness of the bottom came this shiny, bright square coming at us with some speed. I was sitting on a little red bucket and stood up so fast I kicked it over the side. We watched this bright red bucket disappear into the blackness, we then realized it was a bottomless lake. Scared we turned around and headed for land. This one evening we went left to see the area, we were not alone on the lake this night. Two drunk guys caught up to us in a paddle boat and wanted to trade, my Brother refused and off we went. He told me later that they probably would have fell in the lake using our raft.

On some days we would head to the swing. The swing swung over an abandoned junk yard. Dangerous, I never tried it! I was not going to be in pain for a little bit of pleasure. Near the end of that summer we spent hiking around picking berries and realized that summer was ending. School was not too far off for us and we played hard till then.

Chapter 11

Junior Year

My Junior year of high school went as supposed to. I still did not see the gym teacher in gym class. She was also the Health teacher. So, guess who my Health teacher was this year. The gym teacher! She spied me right off. Before this class reunion happened, I had let another student borrow some of my stuff. Mistake! Always, right! So, I got pink eye from her using my eyeliner because she couldn't find hers, I did not know about this until it was too late. And back to the reunion with the P.E. teacher. I know she is going to single me out somehow. We made eye contact and I quickly look down and try not to look horrible. She says "Jennifer it looks like you are high on drugs"! I stated that it was pink eye and she didn't believe me; I produced the meds. Least to say she never called me out again! Smooth sailing for health class, secretly I loved the human body and how amazing it is. Loved health class!

This year I had to make up a couple of credits for bad choices at the beginning of my high school career. Mr. Howard's math class I went. Most of the students were sophomores and we had nothing in common and we just did our work and kept to ourselves. Math class was the last one of the day and usually pretty uneventful, I completed my work faster than most. I liked numbers.

One day I was observing the students and came across a gal that would refresh her make up before school is out. I watched her for several days wondering if I should be-friend her or not. Today like all others she started to pretty herself up and would finish with her eyebrows and brush them up. After this she would put her makeup away and then she would take her hands and go over her eyebrows again unaware she was brushing them to go the regular direction. I finally decided to tell her that she went through all that to straightened them again! She looked confused and then was happy to know what she was doing to her eyebrows because she wanted them to be up looking. I just be-friended Elizabeth, wonderful! I always had friends but at this time I was not wanting a lot of people in my life. I mostly got along with guys and was always with a group of them. Why hang out with girls? They whined, complained and were confused things. Trying to act like everyone had to like them, no time for them kind. That leads to my theory of how groups of friends come together.

Good looking people only hang out with other good-looking people! I have seen lots of groups; good looking groups are not what they seem. We put them in their groups because it is comfortable to deal with. Most of them are set apart, and people don't talk to them because they think they cannot say something cool or interesting. So, only other good-looking people say "Hi" and talk to them. Thus, the start of a good-looking group of people. All the while not good-looking people think that their good-looking friend is out to steal their partner. Barrier! Do you dare cross over?

My friend Elizabeth was a popular gal who seemed to be happy or satisfied with herself. I liked that about her and continued to be her friend. It was very different to be included in the secret society of girly girls. I did not see myself as one of these people. I felt like a visitor in a world that was a mystery to me. I had no boyfriend. I had a couple in high school, but it always felt like I was playing house and decided not to date until I was done with high school. I had got a mad crush on a couple of guys but, I was too shy to act on my feelings. I did try to date a couple of guys just to be dating. Everyone I tried to date shot me down in flames, not sure if I was intimidating or they were just not interested.

I had taken those placement test when we first made it to school and they said I should join the Gifted, Talented and Creative (GTC) classes and get the most out of class and get advanced classes. I chose not to at that time, I wanted to be a regular student and to experience things on that level. My junior year I decided to check it out.

I enjoyed the benefits of the GTC programs, they sent me to Washington DC for a close-up trip. I had a wonderful time. I was not up to speed on the current politics and did not know much about what they were discussing. Sounded like they wanted to put our morals on the line. I decided that politics were not for me and distracted me from Jesus and God.

I did see a real live homeless woman with the grocery cart and all. She was yelling and cursing to herself, I had only seen this on television. The most exciting thing I did the whole trip to Washington DC was I got to climb the stairs in the movie "The Exorcist", so scary. We headed to the George Town University to check and see the campus or anyone famous going to school. First you must go up these stairs, I realized as we approached them that they were the infamous staircase in the Exorcist movie. Creepy and very steep. That priest had no chance of survival after he fell down those stairs. I got to the top and held on to look down these Exorcist stairs. Scary! When we entered the campus, we ran right into a basketball player up and coming. We could not get him and I in the same picture because he was so tall, funny! I found myself in the middle of the Boston Red Socks on a tour of the Oval office. Fun!

This year one of the end of the year trips we headed for the coast of Oregon to Newport. When we arrived it felt exciting like we were about to experience something new. We were split up into four groups to explore Newport. We were all given tickets to the Wax museum or the Ripley's Believe It or Not museum.

I was with the group that went to Ripley's Believe It or Not museum first. I entered the museum to find a mirror that stated when you get older you need to do more facial exercises and displayed the exercises that you needed to do. I stood there and did a couple of rounds of the exercises. Satisfied I can do them I continued on with the tour. We had watched the show in the village in Alaska every week with anticipation. I had seen with my own eyes some of these wonders we watched weekly. My group was getting excited to head on to the

Underwater Sea Garden so we got to the end of the tour to find a two way mirror. It was in a picture frame and said to look at the silly people making faces that were just about to start their tour. What? I was one of these silly people I immediately thought.

When we were walking to the Underwater Sea Garden the place was picture perfect. A small quiet little town on the coast with several secrets. We smelled the ocean air and fish, reminded me of home. The most interesting thing I thought at the time was, it was so clean. No litter anywhere in sight. I decided that is what made it look like it could be in a story book. Then I realized that all the houses and buildings were freshly painted.

We drove along the coast back to campus when the sun was setting. There was a pizza place set up on the cliff looking down the coast for miles that we stopped in and had dinner. It was an amazing time to watch the sun set over the coast. On days like this it felt like we could live forever.

The summer of Exxon was the summer I spent a lot of time to myself. Everyone was so busy working and then tired at the end of the day. I liked to walk. At the end of the day before the sunset I would walk to the top of the hill to sit and watch the day end. The village always looked so quiet and peaceful. Red River is straight across the place called "The Valley of 10,000 Smokes". We could see the mainland mountains, every day one of these mountains had smoke blowing across the land. Some days there were two or more smoking, every sunset was spectacular and different. This huge cloud was like an upside-down punch bowl. Only the rim of the cloud was lit up by the sunset and right in the center was a smaller cloud lit up by the colors of the sunset. Wow! Only after the summer was coming to an end did I think of bears. Not once did I ever think I could come across one on my walks a mile away from the village at dusk.

Red River was a major fishing village in its heyday. Millions of pounds of salmon were canned at the many canneries. The spit of the Red River was lined with canneries and tanneries. The fish were down in numbers by the time I was born in the seventies. We had so many boats show up for any opener to catch the salmon. They were so close to each other that when the horn blew to signal the start, boats would always get caught in another boats seine. You could hear them cussing and shouting from the cliff we watched from.

Chapter 12

Senior Year

Senior year started and I was so jazzed to graduate at the end of this school year. Echoes of what my Dad promised to me before I started high school. He stated that if I graduated high school, he would take me to Hawaii. Hawaii!

I was invited to speak at a conference for natives in San Diego along with one other student. We were to share our experiences growing up. We had a week in a nice hotel and room service. They planned a couple of activities for us when we were not at the conference. One day we went to the five-mile mall, wow! Next day my roommate was sick, we stayed in the hotel and watched movies.

The day after that we took a trip to Tijuana, Mexico. Immediately they knew it was a bad decision. Two counselors and two Indian students with no map or idea where to go was a bad combo. He decided we should just go back to the United States. Good call, darkness was going to happen soon.

I was fascinated by the people and housing. Rich nice place, beautiful houses and then shanty town. Cardboard boxes literally lined the streets for a place to sleep. A town of cardboard houses. Amazing! We started in the right direction towards the U.S. when we came to a four way stop with four lanes on each road. Nobody wanted to go, then we were going, no they were going, and you could feel others starting to get angry. Then our driver just hit the gas and we took off like a bat out of hell in first place. The intersection was about a hundred yards straight. We hit 50 m.p.h. in two seconds to get out of the "Mexican Standoff"! We Survived it!

We get on the freeway out of Tijuana he was so shook up we found a place to pull off and eat dinner. Sun is setting as we hit the border. We just drove on through to get into Mexico, it is the leaving that will get you. All lanes are grid locked like L.A. traffic and a Mexican woman and her children are coming up to your window trying to sell you stuff. Some of the stuff was cool but we were afraid of robbers at this point. So, we locked the doors, rolled up the windows and stared straight ahead. An hour goes by and it is getting dark now. We get to the identification check and the other student says she has no identification. We all stare in shock; you have no identification? The description of this student is she looks Mexican right down to her hair. We handed them my Alaskan identification and the counselor's identification. He states we are on a school trip and everyone is a United States citizen. They give us the stare and silence, deadly silence. Passed it!

I had done more and seen more in the last semester than all of my high school career put together. During this last semester I had traveled to places I never been before, met people I was sure I would not have met if I didn't attend high school in another state. After this semester I had only one more to go and I would be a high school graduate.

For reasons unknown to me at the time I had received a letter from administration that there was a ticket for my return to Red River the following morning two weeks before Christmas break. What!?

Chapter 13

Going with it!

When I landed in town for my flight to Red River my Dad and Betty had a room rented for me next to there's in a Filipino boarding house. Not sure what just happened but going with it. The next few months I spent some down time for me. My Dad had bought a car and was using it to be a taxi cab. My Dad liked to drive taxi, on the weekends he would buy a bunch of fruit and snacks so we could hit the road to explore our little town. My Sister Holly and I looked forward to his weekends to drive all the backroads to get some addresses down. On the work days my Dad would bring Betty and I treats of strawberries, grapes and oranges. Cookies were one of my Dad's favorite.

Day's turned into weeks, before I knew it summer had arrived. We moved back to the village to get ready for the salmon season. My box for floating the river was waiting for more adventures.

During the summer months bears were a normal thing to see. The bears usually left us alone as long as we didn't bother them. Natives and bears have coexisted for thousands of years with this same approach.

When bears were spotted too close for comfort the village was on a lock down. We had to let our family know exactly where we were going and how long we were going to be. The lock down perimeter was between the two creeks, no farther than the school and we were not allowed to go out on the water. No floating box!

This is the time all the kid's young and old would gather at the playground. We spent many days playing politchka, not-it, and cops and robbers. Hours of entertainment for us every day.

On some days Brother Victor would come to get me so we could fish for his turtles and cat. We couldn't take the box or leave the village to fish. Brother Victor picked out a couple of sticks, two pins for sewing and some thread. Brother Victor would bend the pins in the shape of a hook, tie the thread on our sticks and baited them with fresh fish.

We headed to the creek by Up-The-Hill Grandma's house to fish. We had to slowly sneak up on the minnows and cast no shadow. My brother showed my quietly what I was supposed to do and just like that he had a medium size minnow on his stick. Quietly we jumped for joy so as to not scare any minnows away. My brother's turtles and cat had plenty to eat while we were in lock down for bears.

One day a family friend needed a babysitter for her six year old, so they called me in the village. I headed to town to be a babysitter for the summer and make some money. It turned out I had to watch two little girls that were cousins and she had 4 roommates. I had a blast watching those two little ones. We got along great and spent a lot of time at the park. Before too long though the mother wanted me to babysit 24 hours a day. I was a teenage and that was just too much to handle. I had befriended her roommates, they had decided to move into a small trailer on the other side of town. Beth, her boyfriend James and Tom all worked at one of the canneries were just a couple of years older than I. They invited me to join them if I wanted, I said yes.

We were at the trailer for about a month when their hometown friend called them up and had tickets to Anchorage for them. I was not sure if I should go or not. I had went over to get paid for babysitting and only got 50 dollars for my efforts. That helped me decide to go to Anchorage with my friends.

We stayed in a motel for the first month close to downtown. Right away they had bought a car so we could get some work. Beth had secured a job at one of the local adult clubs. One night her boyfriend brought her lunch and got into a fight with one of the customers. James was in jail for the night before they came up with some collateral for his bail. During this time we had parked in a no-parking zone, the car was towed before we could get to it. The tow was going to cost 500 dollars that we did not have. Our cash supply was getting down to almost nothing. The rent we had paid at the motel was all used up but one more day.

With one more night at the motel we packed up the best we could. Tomorrow we were to hit the streets of Anchorage homeless. Packed everything we wanted on our backs and headed out to the streets of Anchorage with enthusiasm that we will be down and out for a short time. We were young and full of life, ready to be successful. A new beginning!

We continued to look for work daily, day labor helped us a lot. One night we slept in an empty travel container parked in the industrial area of downtown, not too bad.

Every two weeks while I was out in the world I would call home on Sundays to check in with my Dad. I had confessed we were on the streets of Anchorage, immediately he stated I should go back home. We have some distant relatives in Anchorage that I could go to and wait for a ticket back home if I wanted to. I had decided to stay with my friends, my Dad had accepted this decision and said he would arrange for some food for us. I had called back the next day to hear he had bought us some food from a shipping company. We headed over there as soon as I hung up the phone to my Dad.

Pilot Bread was in the boxes along with peanut butter and jelly. We were in great spirits walking to the park to grill up our hotdogs. The closest park from where we were sleeping for the night was 14 blocks away. We did not have anything else to do that day and took our time in both directions. Hot food was what we needed along with some candy bars. Junk food never tasted so good.

At night fall we started to hike back to our sleeping spot and collected some firewood to cook up the rest of the hotdogs when we got there. We had the time of our lives living on the streets of Anchorage.

Free, we were truly free. No one to tell us what to do or when to do it. No car, no rent and no bedtime for us. We were all we needed!

Two weeks of beautiful weather, day labor jobs and pan handling was starting to wear on us. We all needed to shower, change into clean clothes along with a couple of good meals would have been nice. We were starting to notice the weather was changing into winter, the mornings were crisp and cool.

I was the most successful at pan handling for the daily meals, I was also the youngest. The people I approached had given me all they had on them or they would give me food. I had no pride when it came to feeding us, we never took more than we needed to live that day.

One of these nice people went to the local shelter to report us. The next day a worker from the Covenant House had brought us two sack lunches apiece. We ate the first one while he talked to us about what the Covenant House did for people our age. A safe place that will help us reach our goals to secure us an apartment. When he was done talking to us we stated that we would think about what he had said.

That night we had headed for the travel trailer to find out we had been discovered. All the empty trailers were either locked or blocked. We walked around downtown until we were exhausted. Finally we found a spot to hide out in to sleep. To our surprise we slept until noon the next day.

Exhausted, no regular job, no shower with our stomachs hungry we headed for the shelter. They welcomed us with open arms. You really don't know how dirty you are until you get clean.

Staying at the shelter we made great progress right away. We were getting jobs, making friends, looking for an apartment and we were being fed good hot food. I was so excited that we were going to get a place before winter. I had been working at McDonald's for a week when I broke the ice cream machine, the manager was a real piece of work. I quit that day! The next day I found a job pinning earrings onto the cardboard backing. Nothing but pin all day, I thought I would go crazy doing this job.

September came upon us like a speeding bullet, winter was just around the corner. I had turned 18 in a homeless shelter. The realization hit on that day! I was homeless in the big city with winter approaching. The next day I called home for a ticket. My Dad had said there was a pre-school job open in Red River that I could get. I showed up and started immediately.

I was a pre-school teacher to four little boys, we had a blast. I had not seen a couple of the boys for a week. When they returned I had said that it was important to attend school every day to become successful. That statement ran around in my head all day. Important to go to school!

Important to go to school! So, I enrolled myself back into high school the second half of the semester. My Dad was not sure, they kicked you out! Do you want to go back to that? He said he would give it the old college try and see what he could do. I was a senior in high school again, yes!

Chapter 14

Senior Year, again!

I started in January and the semester seemed about five minutes long, my GTC teacher hooked me up with a job in Mapleton, Oregon as an intern for the office. I was the official person to back up the front desk receptionist for her lunch hour. For one hour a day I had to answer the phones and write out burn permits. The phone system had five incoming lines and two hold buttons. "Good afternoon, Mapleton Ranger District this is Jennifer", on five lines! Wow! I would have to use the intercom system if the phone call was kicked back to the front desk, and I had to repeat it twice. Lots of talking for just one hour five days a week, whew!

The Grateful Dead was hosting a free concert at the end of August, Mapleton Ranger District was the closest office to the concert. We had everyone and their brother trying to get a permit for camping through our office. It was a free concert for all with a first come first served, no reservations!

When I showed up at the Mapleton Ranger District this real excited woman who couldn't talk because she was so excited, I was from Alaska. She was half stuttering and making a motion with her hands in a semi-circle, she asked if I lived in you know one of those. I slowly said "Igloos"? She said "Yes", do you live in igloos? I had to shoot this woman down in flames and it wasn't pretty.

In my job description it stated that I was to take government safety classes if I chose to. Just in case I wanted to continue working for the government. Defensive driving class was great, I didn't even have a license and never even sat behind the wheel at this point in my life. I thought it was great to learn about the dangers of driving. Had no idea! Near the end of that summer was a wildland firefighter class held in another city up north, I got to go! I really do have a passion for learning and studying. I love research.

The wildland firefighter class was set up for book learning in the morning and hands on in the afternoon. They jam packed so much information in these hours we were inundated with tools and there uses and why fire was fire. Pages of tool descriptions and bad situations to not be in. The one class that made me wake up and realize we are all alive on this day. The hot sun did not seem to be so uncomfortable anymore. One of the worst situations you could find yourself in is this.

The wildland fire is going too fast to get to safe grounds and you have to decide to dig in and use your "fire tent"! The fire tent itself was made of this tin foil space age material that looks like you are tin foil wrapping yourself up for the fire to cook you in. Crazy! First you must pick a spot to dig a hole about your size and as deep as you can get it before the fire gets too close. Then you get in and drape this fire tent over you and hold down the four corners as the wildland fire rips and burns the area above you. Not sure how long it takes to burn out the area around you before it is safe. Amazing! Yes, people have used the fire tents and lived to tell the tale. The instructor took one look at me and said that I should partner up with someone and lay on top of them for added weight. No doubt!

One of the requirements to get the wildland firefighter card was you had to be able to use a fire hose at full pressure for five seconds. 120 pounds of pressure per square inch (P.S.I), hmm I weigh soaking wet 95 pounds. This worried me to no end until it was my turn. There is only one way to find out, right? Armed with the knowledge of how the thing worked and what it was made of, I took ahold of that hose and planted myself to the earth and pulled the lever to let the water fly for five seconds.

Next day was the book testing day and they were going to set a fire in the forest for us to put out, so we have some real experience with fire. What? I guess I did not hear that part when I signed up for the class. Hmm, was that in the fine print? Wildland firefighter class just took it up a notch on the heat, wow!

They provided you with a backpack and a list of stuff to pack in it. Not the size backpack used at school for your books. This backpack was a hunting backpack you would use to survive for two weeks out of in the bush of Alaska! Seriously? The list had very few personal items in it. The other stuff included 2 sets of Nomex gear, this included button up shirts and button up pants that were very thick. Six pairs of socks, two water bottles that held half a gallon each. They suggested to flavor the water with lemon or lime because warm water is gross. You were also required to use five pound each steel toe work boots. I was a sight to behold, no doubt! Yellow hard hat, safety glasses, Nomex gear on, a water bottle on each hip, work boots, my 50-pound hunting backpack and armed with a Pulaski. Wildland Fire Fighter Jennifer at your service. We made the six o'clock news in Seattle for being brave enough to take the class.

When it was time to go back to Mapleton, some of the other employees had signed up for a company softball tournament that was to happen in the next week. They had invited me to go along to be one of the team, sign me up. One of my fellow employees taught me how to hit the ball out of the park. Not that I did that day, but I knew how. Back to work because you can't always be having fun. A week or so went by and one of the forest interns came knocking on my door before dinner. I answered the door and he said very calmly "excuse me but you are wanted on fire"! Excuse me, on fire? Siuslaw National Forest was burning. Wait a minute I live in the Siuslaw National Forest, it is my backyard. No dinner or nap today! I was wanted on fire! I flew upstairs and grabbed my 50-pound hunting backpack, filled my water bottles and squirted lime in them and away I went. On Fire! A camper did not put his fire completely out in the firepit and left. This is the number one fire starter is the one you think you have put out. Pour water on it, bury it with sand or mud, anything People! The wildland firefighters were there so fast that it was contained in the first couple of days.

When we got to the base camp, we were all numbered and given assignments. I had to take two 100-foot fire hoses to the top of the fire. The brass fittings alone weighed 5 pounds each, two of them. It took me awhile to get there, but I had made it. They had already dug a fire line with the brush cut back 20 feet. As soon as I got there it was declared dinner time! Whew! Smoker! I need to quit smoking them things I was thinking as I lit one up to catch my breath.

A week before my job was to be done for the summer there was a fair and Tanya Tucker was going to put on a free concert. Wow, I have been listening to her music since I was a kid. Score! I could not believe I was about to see and hear her in person, so excited. It was a beautiful day and a wonderful concert out on the lawn of the fair grounds.

As all summers must come to an end, we had one last trip planned and it was white water rafting. I had never heard of such a thing, I went! Loved it! We spent the day lazily floating down the river. We stopped off by some huge flat rocks for a picnic style lunch. We were near the end of the lazy floating to the rapids everyone was talking about. We had four rafts in our group to float the river, when it started we got separated a little. When we hit the rapids everyone in our raft was loving it, we were tossed and turned so fast. Disoriented and wet from shooting down the last drop off we came to a lazy drift. Just as I was about to get out of the raft the last group was shooting through the rapids when they flipped over. I jumped out into the water so my raft could be used to help rescue the scared people. It was a great picture of terror and excitement for the last photo of the day.

The following weekend we all just had time to ourselves. When I woke up that Saturday I felt like I had to hike the closest mountain. I took no food or drinks and told no one. There is a road up most of it, easy enough with my bike. As I was getting near the top, I passed a couple and they said they seen a black bear awhile back. Hmm, I kept going! Climbing and climbing it was getting past time to get to the top to get back before dark. Almost there man! I got to a satisfactory I made it to the top spot and took in the view. I sat there for about an hour and realized the moon was coming up. Awesome! I headed back to the place and stopped off at the local burger joint for a reward of wonderful food.

After a summer of covering the front desk at lunch time I come to find out no one understood what I said on the intercom. "Good afternoon, Mapleton Ranger District this is Jennifer"! My friend said I sounded like Charlie Brown's schoolteacher. "Wah, Wah, Wah"!

The school had a ticket ready for my return to Red River. Fishing was good this year on the Red River and I did a lot of it. My birthday is mid-September and that is when the fishing is hot. I got ants in my pants to go fishing one day and headed out by myself. They were taking too long, so I took off for the mouth of the Red River hours earlier than everyone else. When I arrived one of my Dad's clients from Japan was a little ways up from where I wanted to fish. Waved and got to fishing. A silver with my name on it was out there. I felt it!

First cast and hooked into a fish. Not sure what it was yet, the mouth of the river is deep. I played that fish good I thought, about 20 minutes. I decided enough is enough I should bring him in. Being at the mouth the current is racing by 40-50 miles per hour and deep. I started to try to haul the fish in and it took off out the mouth of the Red River. Set the drag for tougher pull and it shot back up the mouth, whew!

I struggled with this fish for two hours up and out the Red River mouth. I was getting wore down. I decided to hold it and walk up the beach backwards. I took like 20 good steps and finally pulled this monster of a silver out onto the beach. Ran down to save it from going back into the mouth, ripped the hook out of its mouth and whacked it on the back of the head for the killing blow. Oh my gosh I did it! I look up and there is Dad, Betty and Henry marveling at my catch. Almost 22 pounds Henry took a guess, wow! My arms were like jelly, they just hung at my sides. Dad took a picture of Henry holding this monster up next to me, the fish was about a foot shorter than me. Incredibly huge fish! The following year my big catch was on the cover of my Dad's camp rack card. I am famous all around the world. Bragging rights and autographs to be given later.

The next day I was to begin my journey back to school for my last year of high school. Mark-Air was giving away free roundtrip tickets from Seattle to anywhere in Alaska. I won! School had a different feel to it now. I was going to walk away with a diploma when I left. I could smell the salty Hawaiian air as I started the first day.

When the school counselor said I could graduate at the end of the semester if I jammed all my classes in one semester. I had only one class too many and it turned out to be gym. The counselor said it might be worth a shot at talking to the gym teacher. I am 19 now and have grown so much, I sucked up my pride and headed to the gym teacher. She stated that I was not to take a regular gym class. Bummer! We did however work out an after-school activity. I was to join volleyball with the rest of the girls, one catch. Apparently, I was past the age of participation for the state rules. The only thing I could do at this point was go be an aggressive fan. Volleyball was one of my favorite sports. I was a setter and a very good ball server; I got that aiming thing down. So off to achieve my goal.

It tuns out I had a class with my good friend Frank, Personal Finance. After we finished with our assignment for the day, I would read to him True Story magazines. The student next to me asked what happened during a story because he didn't hear it. I did not realize all the class was straining to listen to my quiet voice. I looked over and asked Mr. Gregory if he minded me reading louder, he said "continue please".

My regular gym class this year was with the famous basketball coach. Same with Louis, the most gorgeous guy on campus. Man, I thought this guy is going to see me struggle, sweat and run! Daily! Not happy at all. We had a choice of softball or weightlifting. We all couldn't do it at the same time, too many in the weight room. I chose weightlifting. I was a physically fit person, I thought. I could use some work on my muscles. Coach showed me how to get fit and trim with tough as nails workouts. Louis also chose weightlifting.

I took on some personal challenges to be able to do pull ups and sit ups. I am short and would have to jump to catch the chin up bar. At the beginning of class I just shook and strained to pull myself up. Not one pull up, hmm. Whew, that was tough. Two weeks in and I could do 2 pull ups, big improvement. I came to the bar one day and was exhausted from you know being a teenager and couldn't do one pull up. Louis was observing me when he came over to reach up there and did like 20 pull ups real macho looking and switched holds to do 20 more. Wow! I couldn't seem to look away or move, he was right in front of me.

A couple of weeks go by and I hit the circuit with energy today and was going to conquer the world of weights. I did not see him not working out today until I came to the elevated sit up bench. He was a breath away every time I came up for a sit up. At first, I debated on doing any sit ups, but decided to just do it to be near him. Sometimes you got to get some moments in for yourself to remember when you are old, right! I was so close if I chose to kiss him I could. After that I lived for gym class. For two weeks we headed over to the rec room to see our pool skills. Remember I got that aiming thing down. Pool was a game I could break it down and study it good. I learned to take chances because of pool. We had a pool tournament and I won the second one.

Near the end of the semester we played softball and had a couple of heated close games. Now I had one softball lesson on how to hit it out of the park and one softball game under my belt. I got this! My turn to bat and I stepped up to the plate with confidence. Did the famous stick your butt out and put your hands up to bat! The ball was thrown, I could see I could hit this one and swung with all I had, missed. That is alright, I got two more strikes. Shook off the embarrassing spin I took when I missed. Ready in the stick your butt out stance to hit the ball and shook my head to let it fly. I connected the whiffle ball with a crack that rung through the gym. I just watched it sail to the other side of the gym and beyond if there were no walls. Gone, never to be seen again! Moments people moments.

At the end of the semester I was offered a job with the government anywhere I wanted to go on the west coast. California was on my mind instantly, she said I had a week to decide if I wanted the job and where I wanted to go. I had some family going to Renton Community College near Seattle, Washington, so I decided to go there. They had set me up a job with the National Weather Service (NWS) under the National Oceanic Atmospheric Administration (NOAA).

Awesome! So, to get ready for a life in the big city I talked to a friend who studied Tae-kwon-do and he let me practice with him. I had been in training to protect myself since I was about 10 years old with my Dad as my instructor. I was also a master at nun-chucks and throwing stars. My Dad and I mostly focused on Japanese style fighting and shadow boxing. My Dad came back from town one time and said shadow boxing is dangerous. We were to make full contact from here on out, serious? Serious! This is when punching bags of sand started to be a part of our training and phrases like "hurt later", "no time for pain" came into play. Practice was a part of daily life for me. After a certain period of practicing went by, my Dad decided to attack without warning at various times of the day. Coming into the house, eating food, having a nice conversation, making tea and my favorite just walking through the house. I have scars from my Dad's watches and wedding ring visible to this day. I am proud of every one of them. "Pain later"!

I was stretching out and doing some strengthening of my leg muscles during study hour with my curtains open. Oops! Some of the guys seen me and were either afraid or awed by it. Not too sure. I loved the stretching feel, "no time for pain". Word spread fast and in no time I was asked to demonstrate. I picked my friend with whom I had no chance of beating in their eyes. We were going to see who could throw each other off balance. I planted myself good and sunk down into my well of strength. No one could beat me!

When Thanksgiving came up this year I did not feel like being on campus. So, I called the airlines about my roundtrip ticket. I went back home to eat home cooking for that week. When I boarded the plane out of Seattle someone said that I had their seat. Stewardess said she would straighten it out. Turns out this was a first class roundtrip ticket, wahoo!

That semester I had decided to get a job at the snack bar. I practiced making the food until it was good to eat. Nachos, fries, burgers and popcorn. I noticed the popcorn wasn't selling as good as the other stuff so I took it upon myself to make an executive decision and give it away. If people couldn't pay for soda I gave that away too. Word spread like wildfire and I had customers all day. I made more than enough to pay for the popcorn or an occasional free soda. The manager couldn't figure it out. So, he just sent me another worker to help out. Cha-ching!

I had went over to talk to the travel guy and said I just wanted to go to Anchorage for Christmas break because my Sister Holly lived there. I was 19 and could make that decision, done! I spent a couple of days with my good friend Elizabeth and her family. One weekend she said she was heading to Wasilla to help her sister Cheryl to bake bread as gifts for Christmas. I went. It was so cold the engine froze when we tried to head back to Anchorage. Bummer! It turns out that Elizabeth's sister's boyfriend was a camp counselor from summer camp growing up on the rock. Small world! He had mistaken me for my cousin Mary when we were introduced. He shouted at me "Mary". I was Mary for the weekend.

Heading back to school for the last part of my high school career, I was excited. All my senior stuff was ordered and my roommate was going to the mall with some other seniors to take pictures and asked if I wanted to go, I said yes. We all did a wonderful job of senior pictures. My cap and gown showed up ready for my walk. My Dad and Betty arrived two weeks before the ceremony to go shopping and tour the campus. Down to three days before I walk the walk I called my Dad to see when we were going to hit the Hawaiian beaches? My Dad had forgotten the promise he made all those years ago, now it seemed like a dream when I went over it in my head. He had recovered nicely, the next phone call was to a travel agency to book reservations for a two and a half week vacation. Oh, my gosh I could hardly contain myself! I was to go to Hawaii then two months after I was to report to NOAA for my Electronic Technician (E.T.) internship. I had graduated with about ten other students, then the next day I headed to Seattle for my flight to Hawaii.

I took one bus from Portland to Seattle and the bus line lost my luggage, it went to San Francisco. I of course being a seasoned traveler had a backpack of the important stuff. I always had hair stuff, make-up and a couple changes of clothes in my bag ready to go. What do you really need in Hawaii anyways? Shorts, shirt and sandals!

The hostel we stayed at was only two blocks from Waikiki beach. Along the way was the best cheapest breakfast you ever ate. When we were on our way to buy me some Hawaii clothes my Dad states that the swim suit must be a one piece. With my new one piece suit we headed to the famous Hawaiian beach to get some sun, my Dad said he was going to walk the beach. I was starting to get hungry for lunch when I started to look for my Dad. I heard there you are from about fifteen feet away. My Dad said that I looked like everyone else on the beach and blended, he had been standing there looking for me for twenty minutes. Crazy!

Every day that went by I had asked to get surf lessons. Those surfing the waves looked like they had so much fun. One morning we woke up and he said that I would get the surf lesson and he would rent a surf board and try on his own. Yes, we were practicing for an hour before I caught my first wave. We were hooked, so exhilarating!

Chapter 15

Odd jobs

When we landed in Seattle my Uncle Ricky said that the bus depot called and had my luggage. Wonderful! We headed to downtown Seattle the next day to retrieve my traveling luggage. It had made it all the way to San Francisco without me.

Renton Community College is right next to the cemetery that Bruce Lee was buried in. My Uncle Ricky had found an apartment to rent right across the college. I always thought going by that area was creepy!

My job was to start in two months at NOAA, I just watched television and ate food until I couldn't watch another episode. The closer it got to start my job my Uncle Ricky decided to head back to Alaska. What? I wasn't! One of the employees talked with her mother who lived alone about my situation and invited me to stay for six months. Awesome! I was to give her $100 a month to help out with the electricity and save the rest of my money to move into my own place. I did nothing but go to work and go home for six months.

I had no experience in the electrical field so they paired me up with an E.T. to recalibrate wind and rain gauges throughout the Seattle area. Every airport had these wind and rain gauges and every day we headed out to one of these airports. Road trips! We had went to one of the city airports where an air force jet was warming up to take off. Very loud! All of a sudden he hit the gas and he took off so fast up into the sky until we could not see him anymore. As the fighter jet flew past us we could feel the sound waves go through us. Incredible!

One of the other Electronic Technician's decided we were having too much fun, the next trip he was going to take me up through the pass to the top of the mountain. Near the top of the mountain the road ended and we had to take a 4-wheeler the rest of the way to the research center where they recorded the snow levels. When we got closer I noticed that all the buildings were connected by lines so when there was a blizzard they could still get back to the main building.

When we were heading back to the big city we stopped at a gas station and I bought myself a large coke slushy. I was lost in frozen land when I looked up we were on a floating bridge, wow it was weird to drive on.

My job at NOAA ended when the fair was in the town next to mine. I decided to go to the fair as a treat for myself. When I got there they had a sign that they were hiring, I signed up right then. The woman asked if I could work right now? I filled out my tax papers and was given a work shirt, out the door I went. I had to run a booth that had huge stuffed M&M's as the prize, I had so much fun handing out huge M&M's. Funny thing, my childhood friend Andrea with her new husband had went through the fair and we never run into each other. Maybe I was on break! On the last night there was a Kenny Rodger's concert and I went to see him. He was funny, I got to hear my favorite songs and he had a wonderful voice. I felt so lucky to see him in concert, awesome! The next day we were packing up the fair rides and games when the supervisor asked if I wanted to run away with the fair?

A week later I got a call from my Aunt Stephanie saying that my friend Andrea lived nearby in Tacoma. I was so excited to know and be able to see people I knew, I lived by myself now for four months. Two weeks later my Aunt Stephanie and her family showed up to stay until they secured a place. There were people in my apartment and making noise, wonderful. Within a month she had secured a place in the next town, awesome!

At this point I still did not find another job and my savings was slowly dwindling down to nothing. Then out of nowhere I got a job selling acrylic flowers out of one of the carts in the middle of the mall. Awesome, I had a great time selling fake flowers and learned how to use my salesmanship skills. They had a couple of carts in the different malls around the Seattle area, I worked at the one in the Tacoma mall to help out with the Christmas crowds. I worked right next to the art that if you looked at it a certain way you could see another picture inside the picture. It took me two months of working next to this guy and I finally seen the picture inside the picture. Very interesting art, I did not think of looking at it that way.

Spring was approaching with anticipation in the air of a new season it felt great. My friend Andrea said that they were going to drive the ALCAN Highway to Anchorage as soon as the weather allow them to leave. A couple of weeks later I was talking to my Dad and he said that he could enroll me in an electrical class at the vocational school in Seward, Alaska. I said yes but I still had a couple of months left on my lease. I told my Dad about Andrea driving to Anchorage soon, he said if I could get to Anchorage in 3 weeks he would enroll me. This is when he said I needed to do a midnight move. Not sure what a midnight move was so I called up my friend and said I needed to do a midnight move. They said they would be right there and showed up with an empty van ready. Apparently, a midnight move is when you pack as much of your stuff into a van and drive out the back. We packed up my queen size bed with all my other apartment stuff and sold it for the drive up the ALCAN Highway, $600 bucks!

Chapter 16

One way to Alaska

We had arrived in a town just outside of North Seattle, the first stop on our journey to Alaska to get some lunch. I was so excited to hit the road to attend a basic electrical class. Up until this point I had a license with a couple of road trips under my belt. Full and ready to start the long drive to Anchorage. One mile out of the United States border and Canadian border we pulled over and they said that I was the one who had to drive across the border because I did not have any tickets, warrants or police record. What? As I was sitting behind the wheel they were telling me what lane to go in when we got to the border patrol. The closer we got the more nervous I got and they kept giving me instructions on what to say to the border patrol. I was thoroughly flustered and drove in the lane that was repeat customers to Canada, wrong lane! We were instructed to pull over to be questioned. An hour went by and I had to call "my Dad" to make sure I was not a runaway, I was 20 years old and couldn't be considered a runaway. They checked to see how much money we had to get through Canada, I had the $600 bucks and flashed it! Yes! Away into Canada we went with visions of Canadian Rockies and Canadian foods to try.

We hit Vancouver city at night and it was all lit up with fast food chains from America and all the measurements were in liter and metric. The speed signs were all in kilometers and the gas was not helping us any with the liter system. We figured time and distance did not matter whether it was in kilometers or miles, we had a long way to go to get to Anchorage.

It was March when we headed through Canada and there were two routes to take through Canada to get to Alaska. The shortest route through Canada was only used during the summer months because of the deep snow on the roads. We had to take the long route, I love to travel so it was not a big deal to take a little longer. I was not due in Seward for my electrical class for a couple of weeks.

The first night in Canada we seen this road that led you up to a secluded parking lot just outside of Vancouver, British Colombia. We had planned to stay in the car for most nights of our travel through Canada, we were trying to get through in record time. We decided that it was a good idea to stop at the rest stop, as we drove up to the rest area it felt eerie like we were about to enter into a scary movie. We were fearless natives of Alaska on a journey to our homelands. We pulled into the large parking lot that had no street lights and one semi-truck parked but had his truck still running and running lights on. We found a parking spot on the other side of the lot from the semi and went to the bathroom in the woods to settled down for a good nights sleep, we had a long way to go. When we were all in our sleeping spots we gave the okay to turn the lights off for some good sleep. As soon as the lights made the flicking sound to go off we all let out a gasp! The darkness had consumed us and the only light was the running lights of the semi. We were way up in the woods with a semi and darkness. No outline of trees, no stars, no one else around but that semi and pure darkness! We headed back to a lit up area and slept by the road. Creepy! Whew, that was a scene from a scary movie!

Canada is a huge country of open country. Winter wonderland still, it was miles and miles in between towns with grocery stores. We survived off of gas station snacks most of the trip. A couple of days go by and out of nowhere there is a city. We needed rest and a shower, I talked them into to stopping for the rest of the day. Yes, I was going to finally see a big Canadian city at its finest. To my disappointment everyone was too tired to go anywhere, I was not going to town. Bummer I missed that tick off of the list.

We woke up rested and ready to begin the second half of our journey to Alaska. Canada was still in winter season and it was breathtaking. Cool, crisp air with snow everywhere was exhilarating. We woke up in Canada!

We were driving and driving before we went crazy I bought us a hot breakfast and paid with an American hundred dollar bill. The owners were so excited to see American money! I did not pay much attention to the exchange rate along the trip because I used small bills, when I got the change back from the breakfast it was one hundred and twenty dollars in Canadian money. Wow, I bought breakfast and got all this change in Canadian money. Wahoo! I spent that money like it was going out of style.

On the last night of driving in Canada to get to Alaska we come around this corner of the road in between the mountains there was this straight away for miles. As soon as we came around the corner on the right another vehicle going the other direction came round there corner of the opposite end on the left. You could barely see the road because of blowing snow and it was all flat country, the road was only visible because of the car tracks built up from driving over it. The other vehicle looked so far away with only one light, like a flashlight way far away. We slowed down because you could see the road, then you could not see fifteen feet away, then the blowing snow would clear for a minute. Slow and steady wins the race on ice. The night driving in between the snowy mountains was calming and you could see the stars blink back at you every now and then. We seemed to be driving forever on this snowy straightaway. The other vehicle coming from the other direction made us feel secure and safe to drive at night because we were not the only ones out on this night.

We were into a daze of driving in between these mountains that I thought my mind was playing tricks on me. The other vehicle coming at us had only one light when we first seen it and we thought it was a motorcycle or the vehicle had a light out. I was staring off into space at the road when this vehicle all of a sudden the one light split into two lights. What? I been on the road too long! I asked If anyone else seen that? We were all excited at what just happened, all we could do is continue to drive on this long straight away. Eerie! We drive for about another half hour before the light got close enough for us to see what it was, it was just another car. When we entered the mountain pass they did at the same time and they were so far away there lights were seen as one light.

We hit the Alaskan border in the late afternoon, by now spring had sprung on the way to there. The car had been lived in and road hard for days, with the last couple of days being muddy. The car was a mess, we were a mess and ready to get driving to Anchorage out of Canada. The Canadian border patrol had flagged our car when we entered Canada to be searched when we got to the Alaskan border. The Canadian border patrol were real interested in what we picked up while we were in their country. Nothing! We had only eaten food and bought gas to get through the country. They were convinced that we were up to no good. We were asked some questions, then looked at the car. We were about to get a car search, bummer. We got out of the car and said go for it! When we agreed for them to search the car with no hesitations and the state of the car, they decided we can just go. Awesome! Away we went into Alaska, yes we made it through Canada.

I had a couple of days left before I needed to head to Seward for my basic electricity class. I called up some high school friends and we partied up until two hours before I had to get on the bus to Alaska Vocational Technical Center. When I got dropped off my Dad was so relieved to see me get there on time. Still rum dumb and ready to rock and roll! Good times!

Chapter 17

Basic electricity

The Seward Bus Line took me right to the front doorstep of my dorms at (AVTEC). Wonderful I did not have to look for it with all my luggage. The dorm attendant set me up with a room and wished me luck. Exhausted from trying to get there in time to start the class I slept the whole weekend. I had started out traveling to (AVTEC) a month ago. I woke up on Sunday 45 minutes before dinner, timing. I took a stroll through town and decided that I was on to new beginnings.

I had enrolled at the last possible minute for the class. I was in need of some tools, the order was going to take two weeks to get to me. What to do about it until then was heavy on my mind the first day of class. At lunch time to my delight my brother Henry was at lunch and was to attend the Building Maintenance class. Excellent! My Dad had rented a car to drop him off just before lunch because the flight in from town made him miss the bus. My Dad had also bought some cheap tools for me to use until mine came in. Awesome! My Dad is the greatest Dad in the world!

I was in the class with five other students. Perfect size for some one on one learning, I had no idea what I had signed myself up for. I liked math when I was in high school, that helped me immensely for the electrical class.

When I was growing up in the village it was still traditional in a sense. Men did the outside work and woman did the inside work. Simple and effective way of life living on the banks of the Red River's rich environment. Children can go anywhere and explore or try their hand at whatever task was being done. If we showed any interest at all we were given the tools or utensils to work with and instructed on how to do the task. This was how we learned what interested us most. Were you a hands on person with tools? Were you a plant collector with an interest in medicine? Were you a cook at heart? I had showed interest in the plant medicines and cooking. I bounced all over the place but never seemed to get to help out with tools for one reason or another.

To start us off the Instructor asked us to create a complete circuit of junction boxes and conduit. This would be the beginning of many other projects to come. I waited for the other students to get there supplies from the store room and I just stared at the wall of supplies. Wow, what did I get myself into? Electrical lingo I did not understand, sounded foreign to me. Junction boxes? Conduit? Pipe cutters? I was in for a great learning experience no doubt!

They were all guys that worked with these tools and immediately started to create there wall. I sat back and observed. I am not shy about when I don't understand something and will ask. I would rather look silly asking than look stupid doing it wrong! The Electrical Instructor set me up with the necessary equipment and away I went to start my electrical career with my cool tool bag!

Electrical class was awesome. I did learn so many things. Tools! Two weeks in I had received my $1,000 worth of tools. Wow! I successfully learned how to use them all. Being the only gal in class the guys assumed I knew how to make coffee. Stereotype! I grew up drinking Lipton loose tea. Coffee was something you give guests, it was instant. I tried to tell them, but no! I made us coffee the next day and it hurt our stomachs by the 10 o'clock break. The cooking class had started there dessert section and we got to be the taste testers. Yummy treats for all!

Back to that midnight move, they found me enrolled in the electrical class. Incredible! I called my Dad about the bill, never did hear anything about that again. I really do have a passion for information and thrived at vocational school. I did not realize that there were so many numbers involved in electricity. In fact it is involved in almost everything we do daily. Class went along well, in the morning we did book learning after lunch we did hands on projects.

When I arrived to take the electrical class that year all the students that had been there all winter were in for a pleasant surprise. Jennifer had arrived to liven up their spring, I had never been the attention of so many men. Whew! I was not without male companionship. I had to pick the one with no vehicle. He was a big history buff, with a love of the outdoors as much as I did. He was 24 and I was 20. His class mates liked to go to the local watering hole and he would leave me behind. Thoroughly bummed, who wants to go to the bar anyway? This one weekend I headed to the rec room. I found some people that wanted to head to the beach and have a bonfire. Before we knew what was happening a group of biker's joined our bonfire. Biker's and a party are not a mix I wanted to hang out with, so I went back to the dorms for the night. The next day I heard that it was a great party, no one got out of hand. Awesome!

Most of the students were done at the end of May and the campus became like a ghost town. My boyfriend was one of these students and headed back to the lower 48. When I walked past the section that housed the men I heard whistling like they liked me, made me nervous.

We had learned enough to start to do real hands on projects. We had to change all the ballasts out of the lights in the main office building. We were split into pairs to work throughout the campus, I was partnered up with the native guy from Kenai. With ballasts in hand we went to work. My partner had done this before and encouraged me to do it. Not! I was not the person to do the lock-out tag-out, my partner did. I even offered up my lineman's pliers to do the job. He marched up the ladder and gripped the first wire bam, he was on the ground. I was in total shock! Wow! Someone had turned the electrical back on. Ignored our lock-out tag-out! Very important, do not remove any tags. Go and find them, so you don't kill them. Those lineman's pliers were toast! They had a perfect circle burned out of the center. Good thing those were not part of my $1,000 tools. Not dead, we continued with great success. We had to install power poles in a class for the students next year. So many measurements later and tearing up the carpet, they were successfully used the following year. Yes, we were well on our way to a successful electrical career.

One weekend I had hitched a ride to Anchorage to see my family that had just moved there. When I got to the place no one was around. I could see a big stack of mail on the coffee table. I got ahold of my high school friend and he helped me break in. Thank you so much. I crashed on the couch and woke up to my Uncle Jack checking on the place. Apparently, my other Uncle Ricky took off to Los Angeles. They had rented a place on the other side of town. So we took his car back to my Aunt Janet's place. The car was clutch! We barely made it, no accidents! So funny, we lived! My Aunt Janet decided since I was there we should go get the rest of their stuff from Uncles. She sent my cousin's Elise and Brent with me. It was the least I could do for them in their new place in the big city. We hit all green lights until Northern Lights and Fireweed. I am first in line and the light turns green, I try to go but it won't move. I put it in neutral then into first, no success. I tried several times, six green lights had come and gone before I finally got the car to move. Nerve racking! We got to the other apartment and packed it up best we could.

It was nearing the time for my electrical class to end. Finals came into play, study time! One of the requirements to graduate the class was to bend a piece of conduit to a 90 degree angle and a saddleback bend. It takes 120 pounds of pressure to bend conduit. I did the saddleback just fine, it was the 90 degree angle that gave me some trouble. Now everyone was interested in how I was going to achieve this. As I was only 93 pounds. So I grabbed the hickey and piece of conduit and tried my hardest to no avail. I didn't even bend it slightly! Having a time at this my classmate did the Curly Shuffle and we all just roared with laughter. The instructor come flying out of his office stating no fun was to be had during testing. It just made us laugh harder. Still had to bend that darn conduit. I grabbed the hickey and the rest of the class held the conduit. The conduit resisted and then slowly, so slowly the conduit bent. Yes! I could feel the calligraphy pen writing out my certificate.

One weekend a group of students decided to climb the mountain behind the town. Every fourth of July they have a race up this mountain. They run up and down in under an hour, amazing! I could not resist! I went to my room grabbed my bag filled it with snacks and drinks. Away we went to ascend this huge mountain, 3021 feet to the bowl. We had two trails to choose from that took you to the top. Jeep trail or the other one. The other one is the route we decided to take. We hit the bottom of the other trail, there was a rope about a hundred feet long. We were confused and decided that was the beginning of the other trail. We hiked through the mud trail that took you up to the tree line. Three on the tree they called it. You have to have either two hands and one foot on the mountain at all times or two feet one hand. Whatever works best at the time. Very steep, slippery with rock slides at any time.

We hit the rocky part and took a break to smoke a cigarette. Wow the view was amazing. We start again with the three on the tree climbing until we near the bowl at 3,021 feet above sea level. Just about to the top I look up to see the steepest, rockiest part of the climb. Scared of falling off the mountain we took another break to smoke a cigarette and catch our breath so we can be fresh to start the last obstacle. It felt like the mountain went straight up and down. Now we were sweating because of fear not exhaustion. We all made it to the top of the bowl without any incidents or injuries. We were all experienced mountain climbers and new this at the end of the day.

The view was amazing at the top of that insanely steep mountain. We took in the fresh cool air and we can only believe that God had created this wonderful world. God's country!

When we were at the top some other mountain climbers said that they were looking for the snow chute. Snow Chute? They pointed in the direction of where they thought it was and away we went. We hiked for about ten minutes before we come to a large area still covered in snow. We get over there and just stare down the mountain at this snow chute. Right in the middle of the snow patch was a groove that was at least 15 feet deep. We were not sure about this snow chute off the top of the mountain, smoked another cigarette to get the courage up to do it. Then one of the other guys just whooped and hollered and ran at the snow chute and took off like a bat out of hell. He flew down the snow chute hollering at the top of his lungs and disappeared out of sight. Amazed and full of anticipation I stepped up to the beginning put my now empty snack bag down for a sled. I didn't need to get a run at it because my snack bag was so slippery. I took off down the side of the mountain going at least 30 miles per hour, I kept going from side to side up the walls. It felt like I was going to be ejected every time I neared the top of the snow walls. I screamed at the top of my lungs, you can only scream for so long and then nothing. This ride shot me down the side of the mountain screaming. Pure excitement, no control and I flew. It was the fastest most exhilarating experience of my life.

I am a firm believer in things happen for a reason. We may never know why, so don't get caught up in the how it happened, let it happen. I have never had a real plan just a general one. Educate yourself, work, get married, have kid's, grow old and die. General plan!

Chapter 18

New adventures

One of my classmates just acquired a gutted trailer. He said he took the class to learn how to put it back together. The trailer needed to be rewired with new electrical wire, he would be comfortable after that. I offered my help for the summer as I had no other plans. I spent the summer working as a maid part-time. On my days off we would work on his trailer trying to get it done before winter set in. Some of the forestry students had taken a job for their internship at the local forest service. One of them took an interest in me and we did a lot of hiking, fishing and camping on his weekends.

We were camped out on the beach with a beautiful sunset. The next morning when we woke up we heard lapping of waves like they were just outside the tent. We opened the zipper and we were right, high tide! Crazy! We only had so much beach left before there was nowhere to go. We had that tent and sleeping bags in the back of his truck in two seconds! When we got half way to the exit off the beach there was a small stream running down the beach. We were not sure how deep it was but this was the only way out. Slam, the front end went into the stream about three feet up the front of the truck. No going back now, he had put the four wheel drive on when we started out. We lived!

I had ended up getting a three day weekend during moose hunting season. Curtis had went moose hunting the previous week with success. One moose hanging in the shed for winter. I had never tried moose before or went hunting. He invited me to his families moose camp, oh yeah I am going to shoot a moose. We had wrapped some moose steaks in some tin foil that had butter, salt, pepper and garlic powder on it to cook for dinner when we got there. It was going to take most of the day to get to his families moose camp.

We got to the road where we had to get on the four wheeler for the long haul into moose country. I think we were riding on the four wheeler for two and half hours. Relieved to move around when we got there. It was dark by the time we were eating the moose steaks cooked on the fire. The best! Right after dinner we hit the sack because we were going to get up before the crack of dawn to sneak out to the moose hunting stands in the trees. Moose hunting stands and crack of dawn is all I could think about going to sleep that night. The cool crisp air and the long slow ride out made me crash out right away. Before I knew it we woke up by quiet whispers of a soft voice so we wouldn't wake anyone else up. I have been trained to wake up to the whisper of my name since my Dad started training to protect myself. Instantly I was awake with anticipation to get to the moose stand. We were loaded down with cookies, chips, candy and soda to snack on until breakfast was ready in a couple of hours.

We were on foot when we hiked through the marsh to get to the moose stands. We hiked for about an hour and found one of many moose stands. This one was empty, perfect! All we had to do was climb up to the stand and wait in the box until a moose went by. Cool! Barely awake, patiently waiting for something to happen. An hour in of waiting quietly I heard crunching and munching noises out of nowhere, we peak over the side to see a mama moose and a baby moose just arms-length away eating. Animals are so amazing, we watch until they go away. Wow!

We started to get restless waiting for the moose, then out of nowhere my roommate Curtis takes a shot at a moose. This explosion of sound shatters the quiet morning. It seemed that right as he took the shot he was jumping out of the tree stand and hit the ground running. I was not going to be left in the middle of the marshland waiting to be rescued. I jumped out of the moose stand after I realized what was happening. We run for about a mile in five different directions. He decided that he was too far to chase and that some other hunter will probably get lucky. Curtis was not too concerned because he already had a moose hanging in the shed to cure up for winter.

When his family came back from the moose camp the work began. They had over a thousand pounds of meat to prepare for the long winter. Moose meat! I was invited on day two of hacking up the moose into portions for meals. I had no idea what I volunteered to do. The best part of the whole hacking up of the moose was his grandma. She was a cute old native lady with white curly hair. The first time we met we both just stared at each other. First off we were the same height with the same smile. No words can explain the connection we had. I introduced myself and she tried to say her name to me, she couldn't even speak. I said that I would be honored to call her Grandma. She was almost in tears and smiling at the same time. When I showed up that day she was in the middle of making one of my favorite drinks, tea. We had a blast hacking up that moose meat. It took us a lot longer than I thought it would. We spent days butchering and packaging moose meat. We were relieved when the local butcher said they were ready for their moose. Whew! My right arm was about toast!

It was nearing winter, you could feel the mornings were starting to be cooler. We worked on the trailer every day that we had, it was not going to be ready for winter. I started to feel like I had to be on the move again. When I celebrated my 21st birthday there it really felt like I was missing out on something in the world. I couldn't shake this feeling and traveled to Anchorage to figure out what to do next. I hung out with my family and recharged. Good food, company and lots of sleep! Elise and Brent were ready for me to visit. Most of the time I was just visiting for a day or two at a time traveling through town.

I was there for about two weeks when my Dad and Betty came to town. My dad had signed up for a home study course. How to build a building from the foundation up or something like that. This home study course would take six months of studying if you did the 40 hour work week approach. He said they were heading to Hawaii for the winter to complete the course. What? I talked my Dad into letting me go and tag along for the winter as long as I got a job. A week later I found myself in Honolulu, Hawaii.

We had to stay in a hotel for a bit until we found a rental. In the heat of the sun we hit the hot streets of Waikiki looking for a rental. To our amazement we found an efficiency apartment two blocks from the beach. Awesome! We settled in nicely. My Dad had stated that I need to rest for two weeks, after that I was to start to look for a job to pay some rent. Cool, it was awesome to chill for a bit. I slept late, hit the beaches every day to work on my tan. We took nightly walks after dinner and explored the neighborhood. Everything we ever needed was right there in this four block radius. God is good!

My two week vacation was up and I hit the hot streets again to look for work. I went to the local market to get a drink. The donut shop inside the store was hiring. I talked to the owner that moment. I was to start in two days doing the "night shift". Excellent! The lady had given me a full time job that started at 4:30 in the afternoon to end at 12:30 in the morning. That could not fit my schedule any better if I tried. I woke up about 11 a.m. to watch soaps with Betty. Took a shower at 3 p.m. and headed to work. Work was less than a block away, two blocks from the beach. We were set!

We all kind of got into the swing of things, all wrapped up into work and school work. All work and no play was boring. My Dad started to come up with tourist stuff to do on my weekends. My job set the pace for his school work week, we all thrived on a weekly routine. We all had worked on our tan, nightly walks after dinner with a little bit of tourist activities was awesome. My dad asked us what we wanted to see and do while we were there. Both Betty and I said we wanted to see some more of the island. Maybe rent a vehicle and explore more beaches or the outskirts of the city. How did the rest of the people live? I was thinking of fields of fruit, pineapples and fresh vegetables.

The next weekend my Dad got me up early, he had snacks and drinks ready in a bag for the day. He said that he found a bus route that would take us all around the island in one afternoon. What? We were excited waiting for the bus that morning. We did see fields of fruits and vegetables. The bus route even took us up into the mountains that always looked like it was raining. The bus route ended on the other side of the island and we had to pay our fare again. That was the cheapest tour of the island we ever took. Just after we finished our snacks it was time to get back on the bus to continue our tour of the island. The return route to Waikiki was spectacular. We drove along the coast for most of the drive then we drove through the neighborhoods of Honolulu. That bus tour took care of most of the things on our list. Not exactly what we had imagined but the tour around the island, done!

We hit Chinatown one morning for fresh veggies and fish. Then that afternoon we found K-Mart way out in the middle of the industrial section of Honolulu. Shopping! My Dad is a big movie theater person. We took all day to get to this mall to watch a movie after we had Cinnabon, yes! Other weekends we walked to see what was around us, so many shops. One weekend we headed in the opposite direction than the normal wandering around. We came across this cool arcade, Betty is good at many different games. She had that aiming thing down. Betty never made a big deal about her skills, she would just show up with prizes. Awesome! Sometimes we would just walk until we got hungry, ate at one of the local restaurants and took the bus back before dark.

We went to the Mall a couple of times before I found a rack card of what to do while you are in Honolulu. Amazing find! We took it home with visions of new activities to check out like snorkeling, the Zoo, small craft fairs and Dimond Head. We never even thought of hiking up this mountain. A stairway of a 1,000 steps was the phrase that caught my attention. Wow!

Dad had decided in three months-time we could climb it if we got into shape. We had passed a jungle gym looking park on one of our evening walks. The next day we headed over to this park to see what it was all about. It was an interesting looking exercise circuit at the edge of a huge park where they played soccer. We had exercised together for a couple of times and then Dad had suggested that I exercise before the sun hit the beaches. The sun would come over the top of Dimond head by 10:30 every morning. I started to wake up by at least nine to hit the circuit right away, the sun was scorching hot by the time it came over the top.

Every payday I would reward myself with a new cassette tape followed by a dinner and a special treat. I had just bought this cool weatherproof Walkman with some cool looking headphones. I worked out five days a week. Every morning I would stop when I got half way to the jungle gym park and close my eyes. You have to take some moments in life to stop and just breathe. I was listening to either Pink Floyd, Tom Petty, AC/DC or Madonna. I can close my eyes while I listen to one of these albums and remember the hustle of people, the sweet smell of the ocean and the intense heat of the sun.

Everywhere you go in Honolulu there are so many people. On one of my workouts an Old Chinese Man had approached me asking what I wanted to get out of these workouts. Apparently, this Old Chinese Man had been watching me do my morning workouts. I was not doing them properly he stated. I was an angry, in a hurry workout person he said. What? He said it looked like I was just doing it to get my mark for my workout. Gosh, I was just trying to get this done before the heat of the sun came up for the day. The Old Chinese Man gave me a couple of tips on how I would get a better workout. He simply said to slow down. Hmm, Old Chinese Man, better listen. I got into shape in no time with this suggestion. Thanks Old Chinese Man.

We continued to go to check out Honolulu for the next three months. One weekend we went and got our hair done, I got a perm. My Dad and Betty waited the whole time I got my hair permed. They had an amazing amount of patience for me. I loved my Dad and Betty as a couple. When I had my hair in curlers we took a break to find something for lunch. We ate and it was time to get my curlers taken out. I looked good in that perm. We went to a store to get some snacks before we went back to Waikiki. The area was like a deserted downtown district. It felt like we were the only people there for the day. I thought how could the people be elbow to elbow in one area of town to almost no one in another.

On some weekends we would just surf all day, awesome! I never really got tanned out on these outings, I thought I was just one of them that couldn't tan. Months in Hawaii and I was still looking like a tourist. We had went to the Zoo one day, so hot! There was a wide variety of birds, I seen a real live peacock. Wow, so many different colors. Next we came across some real lazy looking monkeys. They were just lounging around in the heat of the day. I took some hula lessons and met some natives to Hawaii. We had a blast! Stopped on the way back for some ice cream. My Dad and Betty's ice cream were okay, then I got mine! I think the ice cream guy liked me. Perfect end to a wonderful day!

One day the whole building was getting the cable rewired. I sat and chatted with the guys as they rewired our part of the building. Betty turned the television on the next day, they hooked our cable up. We found the cable guy and stated that we don't have a cable service. He said he would come by and disconnect it before they were done with the building. Sweet! We never did see that cable guy again. I am a night owl by nature. My job was done at 12:30 every night. That weekend they advertised a Conan Marathon. What? It was to start at 1 a.m., no way! The Marathon was just about over when they woke up to start their day. It was awesome!

Some nights I would just sit out on the balcony with my soda to listen to the people. Waikiki was a busy place night and day. There were no children at night time, that was pretty much the only difference between night and day. On most nights the sky was clear I could watch the stars slowly inch across the universe. I loved it when the moon showed itself, I felt like I could reach out into the night and grab it. The moon shone bright on the evening walks we did down the length of the beach. Smelling the sweet ocean air with everyone going about their business was magical. When the moon was out it made the hot climate feel like you were in Heaven.

So bored with television and still awake on work days I hit the local country bar to meet people. I am not a drinker anymore but they had four pool tables. I met this cute couple that I hung out with on most nights playing pool. Sometimes one of the tourists would ask me if I wanted a drink, I stated that I did not consume alcohol. Most just walked away after I said I did not drink alcohol. To my amazement one fellow suggested we get strawberry daiquiri with no alcohol. We just finished our drinks when the bar closed down for the night. Whew! I was not interested in dating anyone at that time. I was just enjoying being me.

An older Italian man came by the donut shop one day and asked me out to dinner. I was not interested in dating and said no. That Italian man came by the shop once a week asking me out to dinner. I kept up the I wasn't dating routine for about six weeks. He had finally came over to the shop and chatted with me about his life a little. He stated that he was an artist that drew portraits for people at the open market just down the street from the donut shop.

I finally asked if he could do my portrait, he set it up for the next weekend. I was a little intimidated that he tried for this long to get with me to do something. I invited Betty to chaperone the date for me. She was delighted that I would ask her to chaperone. Betty and I ate before we went to the open air market. We met up and I introduced him to my step-mother, other than that Betty never said anything. She was simply there to chaperone the date and not to interfere with what was happening. She just patiently waited and smiled encouragingly. I was so impressed with the portrait. We were about to part from the session when he said that he wanted to finish the portrait. When he was finished he said he would drop the portrait off at the shop. Cool with me. A couple of weeks later he had stopped in the shop just long enough to give me the portrait. Wow! He had made me up to look like a beautiful Hawaiian princess with a grass skirt. Beautiful!

We were surfing one weekend when my Dad said that he wishes that he could pay someone to run alongside of him and feed him lunch. We felt like there was so much to do all the time that we had no time at all to slow down to eat. Just put a request in daily where and when you were ready to be fed. I laughed out so loud, where do you get these ideas?

We were surfing for a while when I finally caught a wave I was sure would take me all the way to the beach, yes! I was flying along the water nicely when out of nowhere this guy pops up right in front of me. I had no time to react and just run right over him. I heard bump, bump, and bump. I had managed to not only hit him with one fin but all three, I am lucky that way. I did surf that wave all the way to the beach. When I paddled my way back out for more I came across this guy. I said I was so sorry, I was new at this and didn't know what to do but run over the guy. He apologized and said that he probably shouldn't be snorkeling where everyone was surfing. Good luck with that and off I went to catch more waves.

Most nights after dinner we would walk the beach to relax from the busy days. We watched the sun set and the moon come up over the water. So breathtakingly beautiful! I could have lived there forever. One night we were walking past the public chess and checker gazebos when a fight broke out right in front of us. My Dad instantly sat down at one of the tables to watch a real live fight. We had front row seats, fresh ocean air with the sunset setting over the water. Life seemed like it couldn't get any better.

Every night after I had met my new friends at the bar was spent playing pool. Two weeks of meeting up at the bar they invited me over to their place to crash for the night. I accepted, I had spent three days at their place. I headed home after the third night to shower and change clothes before I had to go to work. My Dad and Betty were so surprised to see me after the three days of no contact. My Dad thought that I was never going to come back. We were in paradise and I had met some real nice people. Life was just looking up. They were so excited for me to finally meet some people, I had no idea they were waiting for that. I really was into just hanging out with myself most days.

My new friends had owned an apartment in one of the high rise apartment buildings. They lived on the 20th floor in a 40 floor building. Holy smokers, is all I could think of the first time I looked out their window into the world. I am not afraid of heights but it still makes your stomach feel funny.

I was invited to tan with her on top of her building instead of going to the crowded beaches. Amazing view from 40 floors off the ground, I never been that far off the ground with the city directly below. It was a clear day and you could see in all five directions for miles. The ocean with the sun plays tricks on your eyes when you are this far above the earth.

To get ready for our tanning session I showered and shaved. I wanted to be clean and fresh to absorb the sun. I was still looking like a tourist that landed last week! As soon as I showed up she sniffed and smelled I was freshly showered. I confirmed with an excited yes! She revealed to me that in order for me to absorb the sun to get a tan I had to have at least eight hours of natural oils on before I would turn brown. What? Aghast! That is why I haven't been able to get a tan, hmm. I was so thankful to get this information. I had showered every time before I went tanning to look pretty. Incredibly simple!

We had set a schedule of tanning sessions for the next month to see the results of my new experiment. I was always amazed at the view of Hawaii from that far up. I had observed the mountains every time I went up there to tan. The mountains were always in a mist even on the clearest of days. That is why it was always green I had decided. I wondered if there was natural berries or vegetables available to pick. I also was curious if you could drink the fresh creek water or if you would get sick. Some things you never get to find out.

I was finally starting to blend in with the locals with my beautiful bronze tan. It turns out that I did not ever come close to getting a sunburn. I just kept getting darker and darker as the month progressed. The closest I came to getting a sunburn was out on the water all day surfing. Double exposure is what they called it. My face turned a glowing pink hue from surfing all day.

I still kept up the schedule of workouts to hike the mountain. The mountain loomed over us every day and was a constant reminder of the day we would hike to the top. I enjoyed listening to The Eagles or Pink Floyd walking to and from my friend's apartment. The days were starting to run on into one another and turned monotonous.

I tried to get some co-workers to travel to the other islands, a no go. Most of them were collage students that attended the University of Hawaii. My Dad still continued with his school work. It was getting near the end of his studies and the company sent a small kit with the materials to build a little house. My Dad still planned activities on the weekends or we would go see a movie with dinner after.

Thoroughly bummed that everyone bailed on exploring the other islands I focused on heading back to Alaska. My ticket to Alaska was nearing and circled on the calendar. My friend invited me to stay in Hawaii with her and her boyfriend, awesome. I thanked her but said that the man I want is in Alaska, I could feel it! I wanted an "Alaskan Man"!

I was working at the donut shop one night when the most gorgeous man I had ever seen came in to get after work snacks. I spied him right as soon as he enter the store to shop. Fifteen minutes later this group of Japanese came to get donuts and coffee. The first guy ordered and I served him. I did not see the Japanese man was with this group of men. Took me by total surprise. I looked into those gorgeous green eyes, mesmerized I was rendered speechless and deaf temporarily. I had seen his lips moving ordering some coffee and donuts but I did not hear a word of what he said. I finally came out of the spell he had on me. What? That was all I could get to come out of my mouth. I told him he was the best looking man I had ever seen my whole entire life. I had no control of the words, they just flew out of my mouth before I realized what was happening. He looked at me puzzled like that was not the proper response to his order. The man didn't even speak English! Out of nowhere one of his colleagues told him what I had said. A breathtaking smile came across his face as he understood what I had said to him. Just before they left the store he stuck his head around the corner and said "Hi" I see you later. Wow, I blushed to my ears I am sure of it. Sigh! Some things are just not in the cards. He had green eyes and jet black hair!

I had told my boss about the encounter that I had with the green eyed Japanese man. She immediately wanted to know more about him so she could set me up to get married and stay in Waikiki. I just laughed and said that I was going to find my man in Alaska. I did enjoy my time selling donuts, surfing and exploring Honolulu. Every day was beautiful, made me feel alive but I was starting to get restless again to move on to the next big thing. Alaska!

On the calendar was another date nearing, was to climb Dimond Head. I love the outdoors and mountain climbing. Excited! I had kept up my workouts while I was away visiting with my friends. I was in excellent shape, I loved the feeling of the stretching part. The good pain!

My Dad had seen an all you can eat spaghetti place and we planned to go there the next weekend. We had fasted for two days before we went to the all you can eat spaghetti place. My Dad and I showed up ready to eat some spaghetti, bring it on! By the time I had finished my first serving my Dad was finishing his second plate and getting a third round. It was delicious, served with a piece of garlic bread and a small serving of salad on an oval plate. When I was done with my second plate Dad was ready for a fourth plate. The guy comes out and says that we were eating too much. I ordered my third plate and gave it to Dad, I was stuffed! Before Dad could finish his fourth plate of spaghetti the guy came over and kicked us out of the place. You eat too much!

We were catching some good waves the next day, still full of spaghetti. The waves that were hitting Waikiki that day were monsters at 5 to 6 feet on some sets. Wow! Some days it just doesn't get any better. We ate at the open air market to watch people while our stomachs were ready for the next round of surfing. Honolulu always had small shows of the natives to Hawaii. Plenty of food trucks to try different cuisines of the world just down from where we lived. Every day we seen hundreds of tourists, it was awesome.

We were surfing for about an hour after lunch time when my Dad didn't return out to the surfing grounds to catch another wave. I was waiting to try to catch a wave in together, the waves were amazing. I waited one more set of waves and decided I should go see what happened to Dad. I caught this wave that surfed me all the way to the beach at lightning speed. Pure excitement! My Dad was waiting for me when I got to the beach covering his left eye with his hand. I got close enough to see that he had lost his lens out of his glasses while surfing. Whew! The waves will have to wait another day. My Dad and I changed over to street clothes to go to the mall and get him another pair of glasses.

I woke up early on the morning we were going to hike Dimond Head. I ate my breakfast of cereal, fruit, a donut from my shop with some hot tea. I was almost too excited to eat anything, but I knew myself. If I didn't eat right away I would talk myself out of it and run on empty. I felt great by the time we were ready to catch the bus to the entrance of the mountain. Just before we went out the door Betty said she was not going. What? We have been training for months to hike the mountain on this day.

Dimond Head was the classic shape of a volcano that had erupted and created a bowl. On the ocean side of the bowl was the highest peak where the stairs of a thousand steps waited for us. A tunnel directly across the stairway was where we entered into a different world. We both took a moment to breathe in the air, it smelled hot, salty and clean all at the same time. By the time we had crossed over to the end with the stairway the hottest point of the day was about to start. We had been preparing for months to do this hike in the sun. We both were tanned, hydrated and spent days in the sun exercising. Training five days a week. We were ready!

We were lucky that we hit the stairway at the hottest part of the day because inside the staircase was a cool draft from the ocean. Sweet, cool ocean air we could close our eyes and almost feel like a cool Alaskan breeze had come to cool us down. Refreshed we hit the thousand step staircase with enthusiasm. Climbing in long lazy circles seemed to start to mesmerize us as we climbed up. I had started out counting to see if it really was a thousand steps but was under this drive to just take one more step. One more step! Just when auto mode started to kick in the pattern of the staircase changed. It slowly turned into a square zigzag pattern, puzzled we took ten minutes to catch our breath. We were exhausted and the space started to feel smaller and smaller the longer we were in the endless tunnel of going up. Always one more step up. Near the top a very tall couple were going down the staircase and said that the climb was worth it. She laughed at us and said that we only had one hundred more steps to go. Yes!

We come flying out of that small space of mesmerizing staircase to a spectacular view that erased all the trepidation we felt climbing those stairs. Miles and miles of ocean in every direction made us seem like we were so small. We were in paradise on a tiny little island in the middle of the ocean. With the heat waves coming off the ocean and the side of the mountain it made it seem like we were in another world. We could hear the waves crashing on the beaches below us. No other sound made time slow way down. This is what we had trained for. We just relaxed and took it all in. During the war they had built some bunkers in the mountain. One of these were about a hundred feet from the entrance to the staircase.

I was not very excited to go back into that small space where the thousand step stairs were. We had seen another bunker half way across the bowl on the left. We decided to circle the bowl on the left to check out the other bunker and drop down just before the tunnel. We jumped over this small little rope fence to hike off the beaten path. We explored the other bunker all by ourselves, it felt great. We rest and enjoy the fruits of our labor, what a view. We did not bring any drinks or snacks. It was getting to be late afternoon when we left the bunker behind. Time to get back to the hustle and bustle of Waikiki to eat a huge celebration dinner.

When we started to drop down the side of the bowl we seen in the distance a police vehicle parked near the entrance to the tunnel. Apparently, they were waiting for us! Yes, they were there for my Dad and I. Shocked! The Honolulu Police said that it was forbidden to cross over the fence and go off the beaten path. What? My Dad stated that we had seen no signs saying we couldn't go to the other bunker. They were called because people were concerned for our safety. We had entered into forbidden lands and trespassed. He said that we put our lives on the line when we jumped the fence. My Dad told them that we were Alaskans and that we could handle it. The officer just shook his head and wrote down our names for future reference. If we were caught one more time jumping the fence we would go to jail. We already came and did what we trained for, never to return. Jail! Rebels we were, fence jumpers and forbidden land explorers. I guess we trained our whole lives to get those titles that day. Crazy Alaskans is written all over the policeman's face as he gets into his cruiser. We got more than we bargained for, yes!

When we turned the calendar over to the next month a big circle was over my departure date to Alaska. I could feel that someone was waiting for me, for me! As the date got nearer my boss tried everything she could to get me to stay in paradise. She reminded me of the man with the green eyes. I told her I have to go look for my "Alaskan Man".

I have never been good at the whole goodbye scene. If you see me the week before I leave that is probably the last time you will see me. I get the travel bug blues before I leave, I start to question if I really want to leave. I try to stay to myself, stay hydrated, full and this helps me center. I have traveled a lot up to this point in my life and learned that it is exhausting. I was going to go from sunny Hawaii to chilly Alaska in less than 6 hours.

My full time job had made me some pocket money to travel for a couple of weeks before I would settle in at home. Except for a reward every payday I had saved every dollar I had earned serving donuts and coffee. Just before I was going to catch the taxi to the airport in Honolulu my Dad had stuffed a handful of money in my hand. Every dollar I had given him for rent was now in my hands. He said nothing as I was going out the door. I had put that money aside for emergencies as I traveled back to the village.

I stopped off in Anchorage for a couple of weeks before I headed for the village. I spent some down time there and anticipated something. Not sure! I spent time playing video games with my uncle next door. I really liked to visit the old folks. If you got lucky enough they would tell you stories of the old days. My Grandma baked the best bread you ever did eat. I was spoiled with fresh baked red salmon. Days were filled with fishing, hiking and playing cards. We had a slice of Heaven!

My Dad and Betty showed up in May to get ready for the summer. I had been going stir crazy in that little village anticipating something. I was getting restless again to travel somewhere. The need to leave was starting to make everything in paradise seem drab and dull. My Sister with her small family lived in town and said that I could stay anytime I wanted. For some reason it seemed only fair to stay for the first two weeks Dad and Betty were back. I thought it would be rude to my Dad and Betty's return to the village if I wanted to leave right away.

I still needed a career, electricity was not my thing. I had almost nothing else to do but think about what I was going to do next. I had no clue what to try. I figured that I would get my bachelor's degree out of the way then go from there. A plan!

One day before I was going to fly to town I went to visit all the old folks. My Grandpa was so old he remembered me but the days just blended for him. I really enjoyed the time I had with my Great-Grandma Alice. I had spent most of that morning visiting these two elders trying to hold onto a past that we couldn't grasp onto. So many people come and go in your life I thought. I had only been alive on this earth for twenty-one years. The years and the living of those years shown on their faces as I was getting ready to start my life.

The moment I went into my Uncle Melvin's I was overcome by this need to lay down and sleep. When I walked in my uncle was looking at me like he seen something but didn't want to tell what it was. I sat down at the table in a haze. I told my uncle that I had to lay down and sleep, he pointed to the couch. I was walking in a cloud, my uncle was walking beside me but wasn't helping me. I dropped into that couch to fall out the other side into a heavy dream. It was a huge movie screen of my life. All at once I could see my Uncle Charles go to Dad's house for help with his knock on the head. In the distance I could see the Virgin Mary above the church, then the whole sky turned red. Other things were happening that made no sense. In another part of the screen were a bunch of people I didn't know. At some point all the kid's and I were walking down the boardwalk to my Dad's house. Just as I had fell into that couch to that dream I had fallen back out of the couch to wake up to my Uncle Melvin quietly waiting for me to wake up. I couldn't speak or breathe all of a sudden and bolted out the door to fresh air. I had seen my Uncle Melvin at the airstrip when I was leaving and he had said nothing of what happened the day before.

Every experience I had in my life was preparing me for this summer. I was ready to meet a man I could marry. Many, many times I was told that I was too picky about who I dated. Most people thought I would never meet anyone up to my standards. I just wanted someone basically like myself. I enjoyed a good workout on a regular basis and was in excellent shape. I always had a job everywhere I had went. I really liked to hike and explore the outdoors. I looked for a man that was in good shape, had a job, his own place and loved the outdoors as much as I did. Can you believe the only place to find that kind of man was in Alaska, I was sure of it.

When I came to question the Russian Orthodox faith in my childhood, my Dad had told me about what was expected of me in life. I was to grow up with an education, meet a spouse to have kid's with. Give your children a stable home for them to thrive in. Encourage them when they become adults to further their education. Settle in to middle age to wait for grandchildren. While you wait for grandchildren rediscover yourself. Take that art class you always wanted to but you had no time before. Try cook something you would never eat. Sleep at odd hours or simply sleep in. Run with your new found freedom! Grow old and have your grandchildren around to open that jar of pickles for you to make their favorite sandwich. Just a general plan my Dad had for me. I loved it!

I had landed in town with the anticipation of leaving in the fall to a University to start my bachelor's degree. I was excited to see Holly and her family. Auntie Jenny, I was!

I had a little bit of cash still from my job in Hawaii and we hit the bar to find my "Alaskan Man". My Sister Holly and I didn't drink alcohol, so no one was interested after they found out that little bit of information. I made a joke to Holly that the man I was looking for was at his house by a wood heater listening to music playing video games. I was not going to find him at a bar.

The third day her boyfriend said that he knew someone that was single and looking for a date. I was excited for him to call his friend.

I was standing there while he called, they set up to watch a movie later that evening. I had helped them get dinner cleaned up and the kid's to bed before my "date" showed up. An hour had gone by before we called again, the guy's car wouldn't start. My Sister's boyfriend went to pick him up. When he came through the door no one had introduced us. This man smiled at me and said his name was "Mike". My "Alaskan Man"!